He'd ca... trespas...

Out of curio...
Antigua to C... ...s privately
owned island, a bit of tropical paradise that
had once been part of her life.

Now he stood before her in his office,
demanding to know the reason for her
intrusion. "I met you in London, but I
don't know you," he said. "I only know
what you chose to tell me about yourself—
and that you behaved very strangely.
Therefore I see no reason now to take your
word that you aren't one of the undesirables
who bother us from time to time."

"What do you suspect me of? Plotting to
assassinate someone staying here? Stealing
jewels?"

"It seems unlikely, but I still want to check
you out," he said coldly. And with that he
moved to the door, extracted the key from
the keyhole and went out—locking her
in. . . .

Anne Weale and her husband live in a Spanish villa high above the Mediterranean. An active woman, Anne enjoys swimming, interior decorating and antique hunting. But most of all she loves traveling. Researching new romantic backgrounds, she has explored New England, Florida, Canada, Australia, Italy, the Caribbean and the Pacific.

Books by Anne Weale

ANTIGUA KISS
FLORA
SUMMER'S AWAKENING

HARLEQUIN ROMANCE
2411—THE LAST NIGHT AT PARADISE
2436—RAIN OF DIAMONDS
2484—BED OF ROSES

HARLEQUIN PRESENTS
511—A TOUCH OF THE DEVIL
541—PORTRAIT OF BETHANY
565—WEDDING OF THE YEAR
613—ALL THAT HEAVEN ALLOWS
622—YESTERDAY'S ISLAND
670—ECSTASY
846—FRANGIPANI
1013—GIRL IN A GOLDEN BED
1061—NIGHT TRAIN
1085—LOST LAGOON

Neptune's Daughter
Anne Weale

Harlequin Books

TORONTO • NEW YORK • LONDON
AMSTERDAM • PARIS • SYDNEY • HAMBURG
STOCKHOLM • ATHENS • TOKYO • MILAN

Original hardcover edition published in 1987
by Mills & Boon Limited

ISBN 0-373-02940-3

Harlequin Romance first edition October 1988

CHAPTER ONE

THE AFTERNOON before the presentation dinner at which the Princess of Wales would bestow the coveted Designer of the Year award, Laurian Bradford, one of the candidates for the award, took an hour out of her working life to choose a birthday present for the youngest member of her adopted family in Yorkshire.

Knowing that nothing would please Susie more than a parcel of books, Laurian went to Hatchards in Piccadilly, walking there from her showroom in Albemarle Street where all morning she had been busy giving interviews to the Press and making arrangements to ensure there would be no crises in her absence.

Tomorrow, for the first time in years, she was taking a fortnight's holiday—although where she didn't yet know. Robert insisted on keeping it secret. All he had told her was that she wouldn't need to pack much. A swimsuit, a pair of shorts, a sun-top and something to dance in would be enough. Knowing his passion for snorkeling, she suspected their destination was either one of the Maldive islands in the Indian Ocean or possibly the Seychelles. Wherever it was she would be more than content to lie in the sun and swim in a warm blue sea; to rest on her laurels for two weeks.

For even if, at the dinner tonight, the award was presented to one of the other contenders, she could still count herself among the top names in British fashion, no mean achievement for someone still four years from thirty.

Susie Lingfield had been a baby staggering round a shabby playpen when Laurian had arrived in England at the age of thirteen, to spend her first unhappy year at boarding school. Even now she didn't like looking back to that period of her life when the difficulties of adolescence had been complicated by desperate homesickness, grief at the loss of her father and a seething, impotent hatred for the ruthless intruder responsible for all her miseries.

Gradually, a loving family background with the school doctor and his wife who had taken her in during the holidays, and later a burning ambition to make her name as a designer, had purged her of negative feelings of resentment and bitterness.

Now, walking briskly through Mayfair, a tall whippet-slender young woman at whom men looked twice, not because she was a beauty but because there was character and intelligence in every line of her face, grace in her movements and style in the way she dressed and wore her thick dark brown hair, she was thinking about Robert Adstock; wondering if it had been unwise to agree to this holiday with him when she wasn't yet sure that she wanted a deeper commitment than the one they had already. The commitment of a close, trusting friendship.

At the bookshop it didn't take long to select two hardbacks for Susie and inscribe them with birthday wishes, leaving the shop to attend to the packing and posting. Then Laurian headed for the basement to find some paperbacks to take on holiday.

As she walked down the stairs, she noticed a very tall man standing by the counter where an assistant was tapping out the prices of a stack of books he had evidently collected on a tour of the shop's various departments. Judging by his tan, he was an overseas visitor. It was early October. The summer had been cold and wet. Even people with the time to sunbathe had been unable to work up a respectable tan, certainly not the deep bronze of this man's lean arresting face and the long fingers holding an American Express card. Not that the card was conclusive. People of many nationalities used it. It might be that he was an Englishman recently returned from the kind of sun-and-sea holiday she was embarking on tomorrow.

As these thoughts flicked through her mind, the man stopped watching the assistant operating the till and caught Laurian staring at him. His eyes were grey and very direct. As they looked at each other she was instantly reminded of the song about seeing a stranger across a crowded room. So this was what it felt like: the sudden sharp thrust of attraction, the odd sense of recognition, as though they had met before.

The feeling was so compelling that she actually paused on the last step, her large black-lashed topaz eyes almost on a level with his as she waited for him to speak to her.

But although a slight smile curved his mouth, and the expression in his eyes made it clear the attraction was mutual, he didn't say anything.

Disconcerted by the most powerful reaction to a man she had ever experienced, Laurian averted her gaze and walked rather hurriedly to the far end of the department, there to spend several minutes staring blankly at rows of paperbacked classics while the turmoil inside her subsided.

Although many of the men in her career world weren't interested in women except professionally, she had met plenty of others who would have liked to date her if she'd had time to spare for personal relationships. However, apart from a strong affection for her adopted family, and her friendship with Robert Adstock, Laurian's emotions had always been under control. She recognised sex appeal in men, but only in a detached way; it had never had any effect on her. Sometimes she wondered if the trauma of her fourteenth year had left her deepest emotions permanently atrophied.

To be thrown, unexpectedly, into a tizz-wazz like this was disconcerting in the extreme. It took a real effort of will not to glance over her shoulder to see if the man was still there.

He was nowhere to be seen when she paid for her selection of books and was given them in one of the shop's elegant black and bronze carriers. Going up the stairs to street level, she remembered that she had missed lunch and wouldn't be eating dinner until later than usual. As her breakfast had consisted of an orange and a small pot of yogurt, it might be a good idea to have something to tide her over until the banquet tonight. She decided to pop round the corner to Fortnum & Mason's Fountain restaurant where they did a good Welsh rarebit.

Assuming the man with the tan must have left the shop long since, Laurian focused her attention on a table displaying bestsellers as she made her way to the main door. It was only when it was opened for her and she looked up to smile and say thank you that she found it was he who was holding it.

'Oh . . . thank you,' she murmured, startled and curiously excited to find he had lain in wait for her.

Or was she assuming too much? Perhaps there was some other explanation for his still being in the shop.

To put it to the test, she stepped into the street, paused, glanced in both directions and then turned back the cuff of her jacket to look at her watch.

It was a gold Cartier, one of a few personal effects sent to Yorkshire after her father's death. She couldn't remember Archie Bradford ever wearing it and for years it had remained unused in her box of treasures. Then one day in her early twenties she had wound it and, finding it still kept perfect time, had taken it to Cartier's in Bond Street to have the gold strap adjusted to fit her own narrow wrist. They had told her it was a model brought out in 1919, which suggested the watch had been a twenty-first birthday present before Archie's row with his father.

If he had not been waiting for her to leave the shop, the man who had held the door for her should now be walking away, either east towards Simpsons or west towards Green Park. But another swift glance right and left showed no sign of his broad-shouldered back, so he had to be lingering in Hatchards' doorway behind her, waiting to see which way she went.

Laurian turned left, conscious of butterflies in her stomach which she hadn't expected to feel for several hours yet. She walked at her usual brisk pace as far as the corner of the block, to the street which led past Fortnum & Mason's side windows. As usual they were displaying artistic arrangements of the store's luxurious wares. It wasn't the beautiful lace-trimmed silk-satin nightclothes or the elaborate gift boxes of hand-made chocolates which interested her, but what the plate glass reflected: first herself and then, a yard or so behind, the man who was tailing her.

When she reached the entrance to the restaurant, on the next corner, a couple were leaving, and it was the grey-moustached husband who held the door for her this time.

'Thank you.' She entered the restaurant where most of the tables were occupied by well-dressed women taking a break in an afternoon's shopping.

'Two?' Not unnaturally, the supervisor who showed customers where to sit assumed that the tall slim girl and the taller man at her shoulder were together. Neither of them corrected her mistake. She led the way to a table for two by the wall and signalled a waitress to attend to them.

He drew out a chair for Laurian. 'You don't mind sharing, I hope?' His accent was English, not American.

'Not at all. At this time of day one can't expect to do otherwise,' she said, with a smile.

Putting her bag of books under the chair, she placed her small Italian-made bag on the inner edge of the table, propped against the wall. It was part of her new autumn collection. Unlike many designers, she accessorised her clothes so that, having bought a coat or suit, women didn't have a problem finding the right bag or shoes.

Laurian designed for people like herself, busy career girls and working wives who liked clothes and wanted to look good but didn't have the time or energy to scour the department stores, putting together a 'look' appropriate to their lives. The *Laurian* label saved them all that tiring leg-work; and her designs, although expensive, had quality and undating style which made them a long-term investment, unlike cheap unstructured clothes and those of trendier designers.

There was only one menu on the table, which she picked up and studied briefly, already knowing what she intended to order. Then she handed it to her companion.

While he was looking at it, she was able to take in the details of his appearance. She had already formed the impression that he was ten or twelve years older than herself, but as yet there were no flecks of grey in the thick black hair brushed back from his temples and forehead. She wondered if he seemed familiar because she had seen him on the box; not that she watched much television unless a programme had some bearing on her work.

Surely, if they *had* met before, she would remember where? It was not a forgettable face; quite the reverse. Not many men in their late thirties, unless they were professional athletes, retained a sharply defined jawline and a flat, taut midriff. She could see that he carried no flab round his middle because he had unbuttoned his single-breasted navy blazer. The pink and white small-check shirt and grey flannel trousers showed no suspicion of a bulge either above or below the dark brown leather belt buckled round his lean waist.

But it wasn't the right time of year for an international sportsman to be in London, unless merely passing through. And were many sportsmen bookworms? She was inclined to think not.

Not in showbiz. Definitely not a politician. Who was he? And where had she seen those level dark brows spaced above a large high-bridged nose which in turn surmounted a wide and generous-looking mouth. She liked his chin, too. Indeed she liked everything about him from his surgically clean, short fingernails to his navy blue knitted silk tie and the absence of a badge on the breast pocket of his blazer from which overflowed a casually stuffed in handkerchief of dark red and pink Paisley cotton. Had she seen it in a shop, Laurian would instantly have bought it to add to her voluminous files of colours and patterns which pleased her.

The waitress arrived to take their order and Laurian said what she wanted, adding, 'Separate bills, please.'

The waitress nodded. She looked flushed, tired and short-tempered. But when Laurian's companion smiled before giving his order, her manner changed. By the time she had finished jotting the order on her pad, she was no longer doing her job like an unfriendly automaton, she was performing a service.

'Thank you, sir.' Clearly she was aware that her customer was someone special, if only by virtue of his virile good looks.

When she had left them, he said, 'You realise, of course, that I'm not sitting here by chance . . . that I followed you from Hatchards?'

'It crossed my mind,' Laurian answered.

'I imagine it happens a good deal?' The look in his eyes was the same as when they had first exchanged glances. The message was unequivocal. He was as strongly drawn to her as she to him.

She answered his query with a smiling shake of the head.

'No? You surprise me. I should have thought it would happen almost every time you went out. What's wrong with the British male these days?'

'Aren't you British? You sound it.'

'I'm English by birth . . . I don't live here, as you can see by my sunburn.' Before she could ask where he did live, he went on, 'Until you spoke, I took you for an American.'

'Really? Why?' she asked, in surprise.

'Beautiful legs . . . hair that looks like hair, not a roughed-up bird's nest . . . your clothes . . . everything about you, except your voice.'

'The same could be said of you. Button-down collar . . . blazer and flannels, the travelling American's uniform. I haven't seen your shoes yet, but I shouldn't mind betting they're loafers . . . penny or tassel.'

He smiled, extending a long leg into the aisle so that she could see his footwear, a well-polished dark brown calf loafer, recognisably of first class quality like everything he was wearing. Which didn't mean he was rich. It might be that, like the women who bought Laurian's clothes, he knew that the best was the cheapest in the long run.

'So we both buy clothes in America,' he said, evidently taking it for granted that his supposition about her clothes had been correct. 'What takes you there? Business or pleasure?'

'Business. And you?'

'The same. The Americans are among my best customers. I'm a hotel-keeper.'

Again Laurian showed her surprise. It wasn't an occupation she would ever have ascribed to him. In spite of his charming smile, there was nothing unctuous about him, and a certain amount of unctuousness seemed necessary in a hotelier. She couldn't imagine this man kowtowing to a fractious guest. There was something about the cut of his chin which suggested he would have a very limited tolerance for pampered people or tiresome behaviour.

'I'm in the rag trade,' she told him. 'Could we have met before . . . in New York, perhaps? I have this feeling we've seen each other before somewhere. I felt you were thinking the same thing when I passed you in the basement in Hatchards.'

'No way. Definitely not. If I'd ever met you before, I'd remember it. Unless you were heavily disguised by a blonde wig or white face make-up. The rag trade . . . are you a model?'

The question reminded her of Robert's frequent assertions that she was too slim and didn't eat enough. It crossed her mind that the strong current of attraction flowing between her and this oddly familiar stranger was conclusive proof that she ought not to let Robert coax her into a closer relationship with him. Even when he kissed her Robert didn't generate the sensations this man aroused merely by sitting opposite her, looking at her as if he would like to kiss her.

'No, I'm not. I function behind the scenes. I design clothes,' she explained.

'Talented as well as beautiful. How is it that you aren't married?' he asked, evidently having noticed that none of the rings on her left hand was a wedding band. 'Or are you paired unofficially?'

'I'm neither married nor paired.'

She wondered how Robert would feel if he heard her making this statement. It was true enough, but she knew Robert hoped their forthcoming holiday together would develop into an unofficial honeymoon. He hadn't said so, but she sensed it was what he wanted.

'Are you married?' As she asked the question, she thought it was an extraordinary conversation between two people who didn't yet know each other's names.

'No wives . . . no ex-wives . . . no girlfriends.'

Why not? she wondered. But just then the waitress returned and they sat in silence while she served cheese on toast and iced coffee to Laurian and smoked salmon sandwiches and a glass of lager to him.

'To Hatchards,' he said, raising his glass, when they were alone again. 'And to the lucky chance that took us both there this afternoon,' he added, with a glint in his eyes.

A faint blush tinged her creamy skin. 'To Hatchards . . . an excellent bookshop,' she responded, sipping her coffee.

'You don't agree it was luck . . . or fate?' he asked quietly, the amusement replaced by a look of disturbing seriousness.

'I don't think I believe in fate. Luck . . . yes,' she answered lightly, taking up her knife and fork to cut into the Welsh rarebit.

The hunger she had felt earlier had evaporated, but she needed a reason to avoid meeting that intent and penetrating grey gaze.

'Perhaps it's time I introduced myself. My name is Oliver Thornham.' He paused, waiting for her to tell him who she was.

Oliver Thornham. A name she had not heard for years but which she had never forgotten . . . could never forget if she lived to be ninety. Oliver Thornham . . . the man who had taken the island from them.

Temporarily paralysed by the shock of finding the man who, seconds ago, had seemed as if he might be the embodiment of all the girlish dreams she had never quite managed to dismiss, revealed as the only living person she had ever—justifiably!—hated, she let the knife and fork fall with a clink on the plate.

As, appalled, she raised her eyes to the face on the other side of the table, it came to her why he had seemed familiar and yet she had failed to recognise him.

The first time they had met, when she was a child of thirteen and he in his middle twenties, his black hair had been a wild mop, untrimmed since the start of a long voyage across the Atlantic via the Canaries. The lower part of his face had been obscured by a curly black beard.

The first time he had rowed ashore from his ocean-going yacht, *Euphrosyne,* he had looked like a pirate. And a pirate was precisely what he had turned out to be.

He seemed to think her stunned silence had to do with the food on her plate.

'Is there something wrong with it?'

Laurian shook her head. It seemed to her now, looking at him with recognition, that she must have been out of her mind not to see that his face was still that of a man who took what he wanted from life, regardless of the pain and suffering he inflicted on other people.

How could she have deluded herself, even for half an hour, that her *beau ideal* had finally shown up, just in time to save her from yielding to the persuasions of the wrong man? It made her feel sick with self-disgust to realise that she had, in effect, betrayed Robert's trust and belief in her. She had actually decided, in her heart, not to go with him tomorrow.

By now Oliver Thornham appeared to have realised there was nothing at fault with the Welsh rarebit.

'If you can't stand the name Oliver, I have another one . . . James,' he said, smiling at her.

A memory, long submerged, came into Laurian's mind like a clip from a very old movie. She saw herself, thirteen years old and still painfully thin and flat-chested, shaking hands with a bearded stranger a few moments after he had introduced himself to her father.

At that time her only education had been what Archie had taught her and what she had read in the books sent to the island from the library at Kingscote Abbey, the ancestral home which he should have inherited. Then, in her innocence, she had liked the stranger's first name, associating it with the Oliver who had been one of Charlemagne's knights and a friend of the legendary Roland, slain at Roncesvalles in the year 778. But if anyone was the antithesis of a knight dedicated to uphold the code of chivalry it was this unprincipled charmer with his ready smile and total lack of scruples.

The rage she had felt long ago suddenly welled up and she knew she couldn't contain it. If she didn't get out of here quickly, there would be an angry scene and, if anyone recognised her, possibly damaging publicity.

Scrabbling in her bag, she found a five-pound note and cast it on the table.

'That should cover my bill. I—I've just remembered an important appointment.' She pushed back her chair and jumped up.

The most direct route to the door was by way of his side of the table. But Oliver Thornham had quick reactions and before she had taken her first step he was on his feet, barring her way.

'Can't you ring up and explain that something equally important has come up?'

'No, I can't. Please let me pass.' Her hands balled into fists. She knew if he didn't step aside she might not be able to stop herself physically assaulting him, so strong was the force of her revulsion.

'I'll help you to get a taxi. In fact I'll come with you.' His hand went to the back pocket of his trousers and brought out a bill-fold.

Realising that he thought she really had suddenly remembered that she ought to be somewhere else, Laurian wanted to shout at him: *Get lost—you despicable creep! If I'd known who you were, I wouldn't have sat in the same room with you!*

What she actually said, with icy politeness and a glare as hostile as she could make it, was, 'I don't need you to get a taxi for me and I'd rather go alone. Goodbye.'

She saw her antagonism register. But obviously he couldn't believe the evidence of his eyes and ears because, instead of moving aside, he grasped her by wrist and said urgently, 'What's your name and your telephone number? I must see you again.'

'Let me go!' she snapped, through closed teeth.

His fingers slackened but he didn't release his hold on her until, hanging on to the last shreds of her self-control, she said coldly, and loudly enough for the people around them to hear, 'You're taking too much for granted, Mr Thornham. Because we were obliged to share a table it doesn't mean I want to know you. I don't. Picking up strangers in restaurants isn't my style and you aren't my type. Do I make myself clear?'

In a restaurant used mainly by men, this intentionally embarrassing pronouncement might have passed almost unnoticed. In a room filled mainly with women, with their more sensitive antennae, it did not. A hush had already fallen over the table closest to where they were standing, and an awareness that something untoward was happening was spreading swiftly to other tables.

Conscious that she and Oliver Thornham were now the cynosure of a number of pairs of curious eyes, Laurian felt a small thrust of gratification that, if only in a minor way, she was making him look a fool. It would have pleased her even more to denounce him in detail, but that was impossible. Even in her rage and pain, she was not so far gone as to forget that she had a reputation to protect.

With grim satisfaction, she saw a dark flush stain the bronzed skin drawn tightly across his high cheekbones. His jaw clenched, just as hers had a few moments ago when he had clamped her wrist in a steely grip. Now the true measure of the man could be seen in the basilisk glitter in his grey eyes as he looked down at her scornful face. She felt sure he would have liked to hit her.

'Perfectly clear.' His arm fell to his side and he gave a slight formal bow, an inclination of the head.

Laurian swept out of the restaurant, her chin high, her expression as composed as if she were a model striding along a catwalk. But inwardly she was starting to fall apart.

She was lucky. As she stood on the street corner, trembling with reaction, a taxi came along Jermyn Street and swung close to the kerb in response to her urgent signal.

'Please drive round the park,' she instructed the driver, before diving into the back of his cab, half afraid that before it moved off Oliver Thornham would rush out of the restaurant and pile in beside her, livid at being shown up in public.

But the traffic was light, the taxi moved on without delay and a nervous glance through the rear window showed no sign of her *bête noire* pursuing her. Expelling an unsteady breath, she sank back against the upholstery and closed her eyes, profoundly shaken by what had occurred.

It would have been bad enough to have met him in the normal way, introduced by a third person who wasn't to know they were enemies. But to have succumbed to his charm, to have thought he was someone special about to transform her life, that was unbearable.

'Hyde Park or Green Park, miss?' the driver enquired

through the gap in the glass partition.

Laurian opened her eyes and tried to pull herself together. 'Oh . . . go round Green Park, would you, and back this way'—they were nearly at the top of St James' Street— 'and then to Berkeley Street.'

Her hairdresser was in Berkeley Street and later she had an appointment for a special hairdo for tonight's banquet. But it didn't matter if she arrived at the salon early. She was a favoured customer. However busy they were, they would find her somewhere to sit and give her a cup of coffee and a magazine. No one would bother her there. If she went back to the office, there would be telephone calls and queries from her staff, and she wasn't equal to dealing with anything yet.

The taxi drove past the massive stone colonnade of the Ritz Hotel and past the gates of Green Park and the path leading in the direction of Buckingham Palace, invisible beyond the trees. Their leaves were beginning to fall. Light drifts of them scattered the grass. Laurian stared out of the window, oblivious to the autumn afternoon and the view through the park's tall railings. Racked by remembrance of things past, she was seeing only with her mind's eye, and the scene it showed her was long ago and far away but as vivid as if she were still a happy little girl of thirteen.

'Archie . . . Archie . . . where are you?'

Laurian's excited voice echoed through the coral-stone mansion which Archie Bradford had built on his island in the West Indies. He had always been 'Archie' to her, never Daddy or Father. Actually he was old enough to be her grandfather, although he had never looked his age, and it was only in the past couple of years that his thick shoulder-length hair and long beard had begun to turn from iron-grey to white.

With the visible parts of his face burned to the colour of

leather by the Caribbean sun, and his flowing locks and merry blue eyes, he needed only a crown and a trident to be the personification of Neptune, the god of the sea.

Which was why, when an artist had come to the island the year before and painted a picture of Laurian at the water's edge, with her long hair flowing down her back and her legs concealed by a rock, he had called the portrait *Neptune's Daughter*.

Still unframed, it hung on the wall in the drawing-room, the only surviving family portrait. The valuable paintings of Archie's ancestors had been sold, one by one, to finance the extravagant life he had lived in his forties and fifties.

Laurian's mother, Ninette, had been his final fling; a sublimely beautiful girl descended from Creole planters on the French island of Martinique. She had stayed with Archie for three years, bearing him a daughter before being lured to New York by a young man who told her she could make a fortune as a model.

He had not been lying to her. It was the time when American-trained star models were in demand on the catwalks in Paris and Rome as well as by glossy magazines on both sides of the Atlantic. Ninette had made her fortune. Laurian had several magazine pictures of her mother's lovely face and figure pinned up in her bedroom, but she had never seen her in the flesh.

Ninette Bonnieux—she and Archie hadn't been married— had never returned to the island or shown any interest in her child. When Laurian was nine Archie had told her that her mother had died in an accident. He had been sad for some time, but the tragedy had had little impact on her. It was difficult to grieve for a mother one had never seen except in photographs.

'Archie . . . there's someone coming.'

Pelting up the wide curving stone staircase made by craftsmen from the larger island, Laurian found her father on the wide balcony above the ground floor verandah. He was peering through his telescope at the rubber dinghy which had negotiated a narrow gap in the reef which surrounded not only their island but also the much larger one which supplied them with the necessities of life and from whose airport, long before Laurian was born, he had collected the guests who came to his famous house-parties.

Beyond the reef, where today the sea was almost navy blue flecked with white-caps by the wind which was tossing the fronds of the island's palms, a graceful yacht was lying at anchor. Not the kind which Archie referred to as a gin palace, but a businesslike vessel designed to sail the oceans of the world in all weathers.

Her father drew back from his scrutiny of their approaching visitor and turned to smile at his daughter who, at the moment, looked more like a boy than a girl. Recently, in a fit of exasperation with the bother of brushing and plaiting it, she had chopped off her long mane of hair in favour of a less troublesome short crop. Her clothes were a tattered T-shirt, originally red but now faded by sun and salt water to a pale cherry pink, and a shabby pair of khaki shorts with a Swiss Army knife attached by a chain to the belt. She was barefoot, the soles of her feet toughened by years of running around without shoes, her brown toes as straight and supple as nature intended them to be. She was still on the brink of puberty, her shoulders broader than her hips, her arms and legs coltishly long with no sign of incipient breasts under the now illegible slogan across the front of her T-shirt.

'Have a look,' said her father.

He was six feet tall. Laurian had to stand on a box to use the telescope, which was mounted on a tripod. It took her a moment or two to find the dinghy as it purred across the smoother water of the lagoon towards the longest of their several beaches. When she got the craft into focus, the powerful lens revealed that its occupant was a big, brown-skinned, bearded man like her father but many years his junior.

'He looks a pleasant young fellow. Let's go down and meet him,' said Archie, giving her untidy hair an affectionate tousle as she stepped down from the box.

She was pleased they were going to have a visitor. It would do him good. For some weeks past, Archie had been less cheerful than usual, often lapsing into silence at mealtimes instead of telling her stories. Laurian never tired of hearing about her father's adventures which had begun when, at sixteen, he had falsified his age to join the Navy on the outbreak of the first world war. From then on his life had been a series of adventures, most of which she knew by heart but loved to hear told again.

Perhaps tonight, if the man in the dinghy stayed to supper, he and her father would swop yarns and Archie would roar with laughter and eat and drink heartily as he always had, until lately.

So it was that when, five minutes later, the newcomer splashed ashore and, having shaken hands with her father, whom he topped by at least two inches, turned to take her small paw in his strong callused hand, she gave him a radiant smile.

'How do you do, Mr Thornham.'

'How do you do, Laurian.'

Although she was not usually gauche, in spite of her isolated life, something about him made her suddenly shy. To deflect attention from herself, she said quickly, 'What a lovely boat. What's her name?'

'*Euphrosyne.*'

'Do you remember who Euphrosyne was, Laurie?' her father asked her. The Greek myths and legends had taken the place of fairy stories and more up-to-date tales for children in her early years.

'Of course. She was one of the Three Graces. The others were Thalia and Aglaia. Thalia was "she who brought flowers". I can't remember what Aglaia was, but Euphrosyne was the personification of joy.'

As she said this, a strang expression, almost like a wince of pain, flickered across the younger man's face.

Perhaps it had been a twinge of toothache or indigestion—although he didn't look the kind of person who suffered from either. She had seen his teeth when he smiled. They were as white and healthy as her own. Nor did his tall, powerful frame suggest a delicate digestion although, if he'd come a long way and this was his first landfall, he might not have had any fresh fruit or vegetables for some time.

Perhaps she had only imagined that fleeting look, just as Archie had said she was imagining things when, not long ago, she had asked if he were worried about something.

'Whereabouts in Berkeley Street, miss?'

The taxi-driver's question roused Laurian from her reverie. A few minutes later she was paying the fare outside a hairdressing salon patronised by some of London's most elegant and sophisticated women.

It was the sight of one of them reading a novel while waiting for her stylist to finish attending to another client which reminded Laurian of the books she had bought and left under her chair in the restaurant when she made her abrupt and hurried exit.

'Damn,' she murmured aloud, on her way to the cloakroom.

The salon provided calf-length cotton kimonos and several of the hangers held designer clothes which their owners had preferred to take off before having their hair washed or coloured.

Laurian shed her own suit and silk shirt, and for a moment the mirror reflected her wearing only a flesh-coloured French bra and sheer *pied de poule* tights over micro briefs. Then she wrapped herself in a freshly-laundered kimono and fastened the sash round her small waist, wondering as she did so if the bag of books was still where she had left it, or if the waitress had noticed it, or if someone had pinched it. There was time before her appointment to walk back there and find out, but there was also a risk that she might encounter Oliver Thornham again. Which she wanted to avoid at all costs.

Returning to the appointments desk, she asked if she could use the telephone. Having first called the restaurant and learnt that the bag of books had been put aside for her, she then dialled an express delivery service whose motorcycle messengers were to be seen all over London, either weaving through the traffic or congregated in places like Hanover Square, chatting and snacking between calls. She asked for a messenger to be sent to the restaurant.

Less than half an hour later, by which time she had been shampooed and was having her wet hair combed out, the incongrous figure of a leather-clad, helmeted messenger entered the salon, carrying a black and bronze plastic carrier. He was directed to where she was sitting.

'Miss Bradford?' He handed over the carrier. 'And there's a letter for you.' He unzipped a pocket and produced an envelope.

Laurian waited until he had gone and the shampooist had finished combing and placed a dry towel round her shoulders before she opened it. Inside was the five pound note she had left on the table and a sheet of writing paper.

I can't allow you to pay for a meal which you couldn't eat because I upset you in some way. I have to leave London tomorrow or I would find you—there can't be many designers with your looks—and find out what was behind your sudden volte-face. If, on reflection, you feel I deserve some explanation—you did give me considerable encouragement, you know—you can contact me at this number until noon tomorrow. I don't believe in fate either, but I feel we shall meet again. Olive Thornham.

Underneath his signature was a telephone number with a Mayfair prefix, suggesting that he was staying somewhere close by, perhaps at the Ritz or Brown's. She had thought earlier that, in spite of his expensive clothes, he might not be a rich man. Now she felt sure he was loaded.

Thirteen years ago, while still in his twenties, he had owned *Euphrosyne,* and sea-going yachts of her class were worth a great deal of money. He had then induced her father to sell the island to him for a fraction of its proper value and no doubt sold it again for many times what he had paid for it. When he called himself a hotel-keeper, he probably meant he owned a chain of them, not that he had any active part in running them.

At the memory of how Oliver Thornham had played on Archie's fear that, already in his mid-seventies, he might not live until she was old enough to fend for herself, Laurian found herself seething with the same nauseated outrage she had felt years ago when she had first understood why he had gone to the trouble of ingratiating himself with her father.

Her fingers shaking, she ripped the note to pieces.

Laurian cut through the aquamarine water of the lagoon with

the strong fluid crawl which had been the first stroke she'd learned after the dog-paddle of her baby days. In Archie's youth girls had swum a gentle breast-stroke or a ladylike side-stroke, their heads held well out of the water. He had been determined that his daughter should be the equal of any boy in the sea.

When Archie had invited Oliver to stay with them for as long as he pleased, he had brought *Euphrosyne* through one of the larger gaps in the reef and moored her in a deep part of the lagoon, about half a mile from their island and the same distance from a hotel on the big island where he sometimes went in the evening.

'Can't expect him to spend all his time with an old fogey like me and a whipper-snapper like you,' Archie had said, the first time Oliver announced that he wouldn't be joining them for supper because he was going to the barbecue at Emerald Beach.

'I'd have liked to go with him,' Laurian had answered wistfully. 'Wouldn't you?'

'That would cramp his style,' Archie told her, with a chuckle. 'It's not the spare-ribs which are the attraction. It's the girls. A fine-looking chap of his age needs some feminine companionship from time to time.' He sighed. 'I shouldn't mind being twenty-five again.'

That had been several weeks ago and, until today, Laurian had been as pleased as her father to have Oliver's company. But now, as she surged through the water, heading for the anchored yacht, she wished they had never set eyes on him.

She was out of breath by the time she reached *Euphrosyne*. Oliver, who had seen her coming, was waiting to give her a hand to clamber on board.

'What brings you here at that rate of knots, Sea Urchin?' he asked, having hauled her on deck. This was the nickname he had given her a few days after his arrival.

For some moments she was too puffed to tell him. She had swum half a mile, flat out, and had to recover her breath. She shook her head like a dog, drops of sea-water spinning in every direction, her chest heaving, stretching the salt-damaged fabric of a bathing suit several years old with many cobbled repairs where she had torn it.

When she could speak, she burst out, 'You pig! You rotten mean pig!'

Oliver cocked a dark eyebrow. 'Strong words, Urchin. What's up?'

'Not strong enough,' she retorted. 'I think you're . . . an absolute bastard!' She spat the bad word, the worst epithet she knew, with blistering contempt.

For Oliver had been her hero; a brave and dashing adventurer cast from the same mould as all her previous idols, with the difference that they were long-dead or fictional heroes and he was a flesh and blood man, arousing strange new feelings in her. That he, of all people, should be the author of the horrible plan which Archie had just outlined to her was more than she could bear.

'I gather Archie has told you that he's sending you to school,' said Oliver, calm and unshocked by being sworn at.

'Only because you put the idea into his head. It's none of your business . . . my education. I'm being educated here. Could you read French and Spanish at my age?'

Archie, a natural linguist who, at one time, had been fluent in five European languages learnt in the best way, by living among people who spoke them, had begun teaching her two of them before she could read well in English. For years past there had been days when the two of them spoke only French or Spanish to each other. Laurian had read the story of Don Quixote, and the history of the Chevalier Bayard written by his loyal servant, in the original.

'No, I couldn't,' Oliver agreed. 'I haven't your father's gift of tongues, although I can usually get by.'

'There you are then,' she shot back. 'You went to the same school as he did but, even though you weren't expelled, you didn't learn half as much as I have, being taught by him.'

'I learn the rudiments of the sciences . . . of which you seem to know nothing, apart from a bit of biology.'

'I can add up. I know the multiplication tables.'

Like her father before her, in the schoolroom at Kingscote Abbey, Laurian had spent hours reciting *Twice five is ten, three fives are fifteen* until when Archie said suddenly 'Seven sevens?' she could instantly reply, 'Forty-nine.'

'But you don't know how to use a calculator, which is a necessary skill now. You know nothing of geometry, algebra, chemistry or physics,' Oliver replied reasonably.

'And don't want to,' was her quick answer. 'I know what I'm going to be when I grow up. A painter. I don't need to know about any of those boring subjects.'

'How do you know they are boring?'

'Because Archie says so.'

'They bored him . . . they might not bore you. Some people find them fascinating . . . girls as well as boys nowadays. You're too young to decide what you're going to do with your life. No, be quiet and let me finish,' Oliver ordered sternly, as she started to interrupt.

'You're out of step with the times you live in, my child. Apart from knowing rude words like bastard, and looking like a little scarecrow most of the time, you're more like an Edwardian child than a present-day child. It's high time you started to mix with other girls of your age and learned how to cope with modern life.'

'I can cope,' she told him hotly. 'I can swim and fish and bake bread. I can sail a boat and a sail-board. I'm not very good at sewing, but I can cook *ratatouille* and lots of other French dishes. I'm not afraid of the dark and I know how to use Archie's pistol. If he had to go away, like he did once when I was younger, I shouldn't need one of the maids from the hotel to come and sleep here. I'd be all right by myself. I bet girls of my age in England can't do half those things.'

'Probably not,' he agreed. 'But the fact is that Archie's older than most girls' fathers. He might go away for ever . . . he might die, Laurian. Then where would you be?'

She flinched when he mentioned the possibility of her father dying, but she said in a resolute tone, 'Where I've always been . . . where I belong. On our island. I don't want to go anywhere else. I'm perfectly happy here . . . or was until you started putting these stupid ideas into Archie's head. Why should he die? He's never been ill in his life. His father lived until he was almost ninety. All the Bradfords live to a great age.'

Oliver had no pat answer to that. After a pause, he said, 'I didn't put the idea of sending you to school into his head, Urchin. It was there before I showed up. Stop glowering at me. Would you like an iced Coke?'

The heat of the midday sun was already drying Laurian's suit and her short shaggy mop. She had done a better job when cutting Oliver's hair for him. His beard he could trim himself and he kept it shorter than Archie's which reached to her father's chest and, when he was stripped to the waist, mingled with the grey-white curls covering his chest. Oliver's broad chest was smooth and his arm and legs were not especially hairy. There was a boat's-wake of hair starting below his navel and widening towards the top of his brief bathing slip.

'No, I wouldn't,' she answered crossly, adding a grudging 'Thank you' after a pause.

Oliver grinned at her. 'You're being a bit silly, you know. Once you get there, you'll thoroughly enjoy it. You're learn to play tennis and ride. You'll be in the school swimming team. There's a whole new exciting world waiting over there for you.'

'And what about Archie?' she countered. 'What'll he do when I'm gone? You won't be here for ever. Then he'll be all on his own.'

'He could close up the house and come sailing with me. Or I may bare-charter the boat and settle down here for a while . . . help him do the place up a bit. It's in a pretty bad state, in case you hadn't noticed.'

'It suits us. We like it that way.' In her heart she knew he was right. The house was becoming increasingly dilapidated and, by comparison with *Euphrosyne's* spick and span order, untidy and not very clean. But both she and Archie had more interesting things to do with their time than spend it sweeping and banishing cobwebs and cockroaches from the rooms no longer in use.

Having refused his offer of a chilled Coke, she wished she could change her mind. The strenuous swim had made her thirsty. Her head ached and low down in her tummy there was another ache which, on and off, had been there for some days. She had felt oddly out of sorts before Archie dropped his bombshell. Now, all at once, she felt like bursting into tears.

'Oh . . . why don't you go away and leave us alone? We don't want you here . . . interfering . . . changing things!' Laurian cried angrily.

Unable to stand the sight of him a minute more, she dived back into the sea and swam back the way she had come.

Later in the day she felt a stickiness between her legs and,

investigating, found she was bleeding. It wasn't a shock:
Archie had told her what to expect. Now she wasn't a child
any more but a woman. She could have a baby. On that
subject her father had been less direct and matter-of-fact. He
had said she would find all she wanted to know in the medical
encyclopaedia, a forty-year-old volume which was more
explanatory about snake bites and accidental poisonings than
about what making love meant.

A few days ago she had debated asking Oliver to explain
certain things which puzzled her. A few days ago she had
thought she was in love with him, and had wondered how long
it would be before she was grown up enough for him to fall in
love with her. Sixteen? Seventeen? But would he still be
around then?

How different her feelings were now. She felt he had
betrayed her; was convinced that it *had* been his idea to send
her away to cold, wet, desolate England.

Remembering that long-ago day as another taxi took her from
the hairdressers to the house she shared with Robert Adstock,
Laurian could concede, in retrospect, that everything Oliver
had said had been true.

Within a year of leaving the island she had been beginning
to enjoy her new life among girls of her own age; and certainly,
without some formal education and good grades at O and A
levels, she would never have been accepted by the Royal
College of Art.

What she could not forgive was Oliver's real reason for
convincing Archie that he must send her away. Far from
putting on pressure out of a disinterested concern for her
welfare, Oliver had been motivated by avaricious self-interest.
He had known the island was a potential goldmine and had
bought it, if not for a song, for far below its market value.

In taking her home, the taxi passed through the City, the financial heart of London, where in a few hours' time Laurian and Robert would be dining in the historic surroundings of the hall of one of the City's most ancient Guilds.

Spitalfields, where they lived, was a part of the former East End, an area where, until comparatively recently, only poor people had lived. Now, like much of London's disused dockland, their part of the old East End was one of the newest 'in' places to live.

She and Robert and three other art students had acquired their dilapidated silk-weaver's house when only a discerning few recognised the charm and convenience of the Spitalfields area. Between them they had put the building to rights, each having one room of their own and sharing the bathroom and kitchen.

Then one of the three young men who made up their commune had been offered a job in New York and the others had decided to put in another kitchen and bathroom, converting the house into flats. Laurian and Candida had had the top floors and Robert and Pete had lived below them.

That arrangement had ended with Candida's marriage to a New Zealander, since when Pete had departed, leaving Robert and Laurian the sole occupants.

The panelled hall and beautiful eighteenth-century staircase were still shared. As Laurian put away her latch-key and turned to the hall table to see if there was any mail for her, the door behind her opened and a fair-haired man in his early thirties appeared.

'How about a drink before you go up to change?' he asked. 'Your hair looks marvellous. But you look a bit drained, dear girl. Has it been a tough day? Come and relax for half an hour.'

'Hello, Robert.' A smile lit up Laurian's face as he beckoned her into his living-room. She held up the bag of books. 'Paperbacks for our journey and the beach. I got a couple for you.' Her conscience pricked her as she remembered how, for a short time, she had been ready to back out of the holiday.

'Thanks. That was thoughtful of you. I may buy some more at Heathrow—they get the big bestsellers before they come out in the shops. What'll you have? G and T?'

She shook her head. 'Just tonic for me. Gin would go straight to my head—I missed lunch. I'd better have something to eat before I drink any alcohol.'

'I'll fix you a cold beef sandwich. Sit down and put your feet up.' He shoved her gently towards one end of his sofa and, when she was seated, scooped her legs up by the ankles to take off her low-heeled court shoes and put her feet on the sofa. 'You push yourself too hard. You should have taken the day off and rested before your big night.'

When he had gone to the kitchen, Laurian expelled a long sigh and consciously relaxed all her muscles. Not that tension was normally one of her problems. She *did* push herself, as Robert said, but then so did he. They were both workaholics; partly, perhaps, because they had no private lives to speak of.

Robert was a design consultant whose most important client was a chain of High Street shops for whom he had re-designed their image so effectively that their shares had rocketed. However, there were many equally successful consultancies fighting for the plum contracts from the major retailers. Robert's firm would only prosper as long as he and his team could continue to repeat the brilliant face-lifts which were needed every few years to keep each chain abreast of its rivals.

One of the things which worried Laurian about a partnership with him was that while they seldom stopped talking when they were together and had many interests in common, their approach to interior decoration was totally dissimilar.

Robert was a modernist whose decor changed with every new trend. She was a traditionalist. His part of the house was done out in stark black and white with mainly art deco furniture, and surrealist paintings Laurian knew she couldn't live with. Her rooms upstairs were quite different; antique furniture, traditional English chintzes, pot plants and sometimes in summer bunches of cut flowers sent down from the Yorkshire garden of her adopted family, and everywhere books and stacks of fashion magazines.

Robert returned with a plate of sandwiches and a tall glass of milk.

'There's no better lining for an empty stomach,' he said, pushing a low chrome and glass table on wheels towards the sofa. 'Are you all packed and ready to take off tomorrow?'

She nodded. 'I packed last night. How was your day?'

He told her, and Laurian listened with genuine interest, for their careers, although in different fields, had many things in common.

'I ran into Celie in Oxford Street this morning,' he added, as an afterthought. 'She's looking well.'

Laurian knew all about his ex-wife, Cecilia, who had been the girl next door and whom he had married at nineteen, under pressure from both their families when Celie found herself pregnant.

They both came from a small northern town where engagements and white weddings were still the norm. Celie had come south with Robert, but their marriage had been a mistake. Two years later she had met someone else, an older man whose wife had deserted him and who needed someone to look after him and his teenage son in their comfortable bungalow in one of London's dormitory suburbs. Now Celia had another child by her second husband and Robert's daughter regarded her stepfather as her real father and Robert as a kind of uncle whom she liked but didn't see often. It wasn't a situation which caused him any pain. He was glad a youthful mistake had turned out well for everyone concerned. Perhaps put off by his first experience of fatherhood, he didn't intend to have any more children.

This was something else which troubled Laurian. The five years of school holidays she had spent in the bosom of Dr and Mrs Lingfield's large and united family had made her hope to emulate them one day.

It was on the tip of her tongue to tell Robert that she, too, had run into someone from her past today, but before she could do so, he went on, 'I told her about tonight. She wanted to know what you were wearing, but I couldn't say.'

'Well, as you're keeping me in suspense about where we're going tomorrow, you'll have to wait till later to see my *grande toilette*. Actually I haven't gone overboard in case I'm one of the also-rans.'

'You're going to win it. No doubt about that,' he assured her. 'I wonder what Diana will wear? Nothing by anyone on the short list, presumably?'

'I shouldn't think so, unless she decided to wear something by the winner. I'm sure she'll know in advance who it's going to be.

'I'd better go and have my bath,' she said, her energy revived by the milk and sandwiches. 'It will take me longer than usual to do my face. I'll be down again at seven sharp.'

'OK. See you later. If you want any help with your zip or whatever, just give me a ring,' said Robert, crossing the room to open the door for her.

'Thanks.' She gave his arm an affectionate squeeze on her way out.

Presently, as she lay in scented, not too hot water, her hair protected by a loose turban of tulle, it wasn't her holiday with

Robert or the important evening ahead which occupied her thoughts.

Unwillingly, she found herself thinking of Oliver Thornham and of the note he had written to her. Even though she had torn it up, she could remember the telephone number. But although, now, she rather regretted not telling him in the restaurant precisely why she despised him, she had no intention of doing it by telephone. Not only because there wasn't time, and she didn't want to get steamed up again before the banquet, but also because she felt it would irritate him more not to know why a woman who had seemed to be succumbing to his charm had suddenly walked out on him.

. . . *I feel we shall meet again,* he had written.

Not if I see you first, she thought. And forced herself to concentrate on rehearsing what to say if she won the Award and what if she didn't.

CHAPTER TWO

'YOU LOOKED wonderful . . . you *feel* wonderful.' Robert's fingers smoothed the soft pile encasing Laurian's slim arm.

The banquet was over. A taxi was taking them home. His arm was around her and she was leaning against his shoulder, the excitement and elation of her triumph dying down now and exhaustion beginning to set in.

'That's because it's silk velvet,' she told him, as he went on gently stroking her. 'It was always used for good clothes up to the Second World War, and then other fibres took over which don't have the same supple feel. This dress is made from a bolt of 1930s ring velvet I bought in an antiques market when I first came to London. I've been saving it for a special occasion.'

'There'll never be a more special one than tonight. The Princess looked a knock-out, and so did you. It was clever of you to wear something very simple to contrast with the drop-dead number you designed for her.'

'I was thrilled that she wore it,' said Laurian. 'The silk for the top was another piece from my hoard of old fabrics.'

'Everyone was talking about your fantastic colour sense,' Robert told her.

'The credit belongs to whoever designed the pattern on the silk,' Laurian said candidly.

She had bought it at a country house auction during the last summer holiday before she left school. It was Barbara Lingfield, her foster-mother, who had introduced Laurian to

37

the fun of auctions. On that occasion nobody else had been interested in a few yards of vivid French silk rolled on a cardboard tube and interleaved with tissue paper which had protected the delicate threads from deteriorating.

Patterned with blue hydrangea heads and sprays of purple lilac on a golden orange ground, it hadn't appealed to the conservative tastes of the women at the auction view.

'Tangerine and purple . . . what a horrible clash!' she remembered hearing someone say. But even before her training in fashion design, Laurian had recognised that the three strong colours combined to give a wonderful vibrancy.

For the dress which the Princess of Wales had worn at the banquet tonight, she had had the silk made into a plain close-fitting bodice with muttonchop sleeves and the whole top covered with colourless transparent sequins which added a subtle shimmer to the rich pattern. The skirt was plain; yards of lustrous golden-orange taffeta with a sash of dark lilac satin tied in a bow at the front of the Princess's waist. She had looked even more glamorous than usual and there had been much speculation about the designer of the dress.

Later, before announcing who had won, she had said she was wearing a dress by the winner. Then, in a tense hush, she had called Laurian up to receive the Award.

'I was very proud of you tonight,' Robert told her, his arm tightening round her. 'You looked so calm and composed . . . and very beautiful.'

'Thank you. I'm glad I *looked* calm. I didn't feel it. I was quaking with nervousness inwardly.'

'I did notice you only pecked at your dinner. Are you hungry now it's all over? Shall I make you a toasted cheese sandwich?'

Laurian shook her head, smiling at his eagerness to feed her. 'I ate quite enough to keep body and soul together. Resign yourself, Robert; I'm never going to be a plump, cosy armful, so you might as well give up the struggle to fatten me up.'

'I don't want to. You're fine as you are. As the woman next to me remarked, only a girl with a perfect figure could wear this dress.'

They were sitting in the corner of the cab which was not reflected in the driver's rear-view mirror, and suddenly Robert began to make love to her, nuzzling her cheek with his lips, his other hand stroking her thigh.

These caresses were still very gentle, tentative even, as if he were waiting for some indication from her that this was what she wanted to happen. Up to a point, she did. What kept her from leaning her head back and letting him find her lips was the thought that it wouldn't stop at a few tender kisses; and although she was glad of his affection, the evening—indeed the whole day—had taken too much out of her for her to be capable of responding to passion.

'You always smell so good,' he murmured, sniffing the fragrant place behind her left ear which, several hours earlier, she had dabbed with *Amour Amour,* the first scent created, and recently revived by the house which still bore his name, by the designer who had most influenced her. The Frenchman, Jean Patou.

'Dear Robert . . . will you think me an awful drag if, when we get back, I forgo that champagne nightcap,'— convinced she would win, he had left a bottle on ice to await their return— 'and totter straight up to bed? It's been quite a taxing week, what with Monday and everything.' She had shown her Collection for next spring at the beginning of the week. 'If I've got to get up fairly early, I think I should hit the hay.'

He stopped exploring her neck and withdrew his hand

from her leg.

'Yes, of course . . . you do that,' he said.

She could tell he was disappointed, had been hoping the evening might end with them both in his bed.

She felt guilty, and vexed by the feeling. After all, she had made it clear, when the holiday was mooted, that he shouldn't take anything for granted. They were neighbours and long-time friends, and a holiday was always more enjoyable with a congenial companion. It would be a chance to test how they liked being together all day for two weeks at a stretch. But they wouldn't be sharing a room, at least not at the outset. That had been quite clearly stated, and Robert had understood that he was to book separate bedrooms.

Perhaps she ought not have let him hug her; but how could she have prevented it without seeming absurdly prim? Anyway, she had liked his arm round her. It was possible, even probable, that in a few days' time, when she was feeling rested, she would want to be made love to. But not tonight. Not right on top of a major public appearance, with the eyes of the fashion world upon her, not to mention press and television cameras. It had been a wonderful boost to her career and she seemed to have acquitted herself satisfactorily. But she hadn't actually *enjoyed* being in the spotlight. It had confirmed that she was basically a private person, not a natural celebrity, loving every moment of limelight.

The taxi drew up at their front door. Robert jumped out and turned to help her alight. While he paid the driver, Laurian took out the key which from force of habit she had transferred to the small chestnut velvet envelope, lined with gold kid, which matched her dress.

Robert followed her into the house and closed and bolted the door.

Her hand on the curl of the banister rail, one foot on the

bottom stair, she turned. 'I couldn't have had a more distinguished, nicer-looking escort. Thank you for going with me, Robert. You were a tremendous support.'

'I wouldn't have missed it.' He came to where she was standing, a lock of his fair hair beginning to fall across his forehead. He had given a touch of individuality to his dinner jacket and wing-collared dress shirt by wearing a bow tie of pewter silk in place of the conventional black grosgrain.

The silk was the exact colour of Oliver Thornham's eyes; a disturbing reminder, which Laurian had striven to ignore, of her upsetting encounter with him.

'I'm going to kiss you goodnight,' Robert told her, and took her firmly in his arms.

He had kissed her a few times before, in a light-hearted friendly way, but this time his mouth covered hers for what seemed a long time as he tried to rouse a response. She sensed his loneliness, his hunger for physical love. It was several months since he had broken off a long liaison with an older woman, and Laurian was sure there had been no one else since then. Robert wasn't a womaniser. She wouldn't have liked him if he had been.

Although she yielded to his embrace, Laurian's lips remained passive under his.

He let her go. 'Don't forget to set your alarm. Sleep well. Goodnight.'

He waited until she reached the bend of the staircase and then, with a lift of the hand as she looked down at him, he turned and moved out of sight.

When the alarm went next morning, she stretched out an arm to switch it off and then snuggled back under the soft warm duvet, its cover appliquéd, to her design, with a trellis of pale blue ribbons, here and there tied in bows.

Her bedroom was the garret at the top of the house where the Huguenot silk weavers—Protestant refugees from persecution in France—had worked at their looms, creating exquisite silks to be worn by the English aristocracy. The garret was the lightest room in the house and Laurian always opened the curtains last thing at night in order to be woken by the sun—when it wasn't obscured by the clouds which hung over London on so many days of the year.

She still missed the Caribbean sun and the warm, crystalline sea. Three times a week she swam at a private club to keep her muscles in tone, but it was a necessary exercise, not a joy.

In spite of her fatigue last night, she hadn't slept deeply. She remembered a long, confused dream about arriving at the banquet with only one shoe. This had merged with another sequence in which Robert, despite her protests, had tried to make love to her on an aeroplane until the stewardess had called the Captain to deal with him. The Captain had been Oliver Thornham.

She hadn't been awake long when the telephone rang.

'Hello?' She expected to hear Robert's voice, checking that she hadn't overslept.

'Laurian dear . . . congratulations! It was on the early news. I'm so pleased . . . and so very proud of you.' It was her foster-mother calling from Yorkshire.

'Hello, Ma. I was going to ring you later.'

Like the Lingfields' four children, Laurian spoke and thought of Barbara as 'Ma', and loved her as dearly as if she were her real mother. A kind, understanding housemistress at her boarding school, and Dr Lingfield's wife, she had been the first feminine influences in her life, supporting her through that appalling first year when, exiled from everything familiar and separated by an ocean from her adored father, next she had suffered the anguish of being told he had died.

After wanting to hear all the details of the presentation, Mrs Lingfield said, 'Bill isn't here at the moment. He's at a confinement . . . a girl who insisted on having her baby at home. I expect he'll ring you when he comes in. Are you still going on this holiday with Robert Adstock?'

Laurian knew that Ma, although the least narrow-minded of women, didn't really approve of modern manners and morals. She believed it was wiser to make up one's mind about a man before setting up home with him. However, when Jenny, her eldest daughter, had asked if her parents had slept together before their wedding, Mrs Lingfield had been honest enough to admit that they had.

'I think most people did—once they were engaged and if the opportunity was offered,' she had said frankly. 'It was before the Pill and lots of girls suffered terrible anxiety every month in case they were pregnant. Fortunately, Bill being a medical student and more clued up than most young men, I didn't have that worry . . . or only once when my period was late for some reason. Anyway, it wouldn't have mattered. We were desperately in love and due to be married quite soon.'

In answer to Mrs Lingfield's question, Laurian said, 'Our flight takes off at ten, but I still don't know where we're going. Robert insists on keeping it a magical mystery tour. I know you don't like the idea, Ma, but please don't worry about it.'

'My dear, you're a grown-up woman and must run your own life. I have no right to interfere . . . or even to offer advice. It's just that I'd like all my girls to have what I had . . . the bliss of being in love.'

'Being in love so often ends in tears,' said Laurian, thinking of all the girls she had known whose love affairs hadn't prospered.

'Not if it's real love, as opposed to infatuation,' said Barbara Lingfield, not for the first time. 'The important thing is to ask oneself: is he kind? Does he make me laugh? Do we have plenty to talk about when we're not in each other's arms?'

'Robert *is* kind. We have masses to talk about. We never stop.'

Laurian couldn't claim that he made her laugh, although occasionally he would pass on a joke he had heard someone else tell. Anyway, jokes, as such, were not what her foster-mother meant. The Lingfield family all had a highly developed sense of the ridiculous and were capable of falling about at things which wouldn't seem hilarious to other people. Laurian had laughed more in her years with them than she ever had before or since.

'Yes, you do have a lot in common, but you aren't in love with him, Laurie. He doesn't make the sun shine for you, regardless of the weather in the streets. Bill still does that for me. Not all the time—we have our ups and downs. But on the rare occasions when we're apart, I still can't wait to get back to him . . . and that's after thirty-three years. Some people *do* live happily ever after, my dear, whatever the cynics may say about the rising divorce rate.'

'I know, Ma—and you and Pa are living proof that true love does last for ever. But you did have to make a choice between marriage and your career. And, as you've often said, one can't have everything in life. I have lashings of job-fulfilment. It would be asking a lot to expect a great love as well. Look, still in bed and it's time I was up. Bless you for calling. I'll send you a p.c. as soon as we get to wherever we're going.'

When they had said goodbye, Laurian switched on her answering machine, already primed with a message asking callers to try her office number after nine o'clock. She had anticipated that today a lot of people would ring up to congratulate or commiserate with her. Her secretary would explain that she would be incommunicado for the next two weeks.

In some ways it was not very convenient to be leaving town the morning after the presentation. She knew that she would have been on *Wogan* tonight, had she been staying in London. It wasn't a personal disappointment to miss being interviewed on Britain's premier chat show, but her backers would think she had let slip an important opportunity to promote the *Laurian* label in front of a huge audience. Not to worry. The show might still want her when she came back.

Passing the chestnut velvet dress which was hanging on the outside of one of her clothes cupboard doors, she hurried into the bathroom for a quick shower.

'Mr Adstock, your secretary is on the telephone. It sounds rather urgent.'

Robert had lowered his newspaper when the ground stewardess approached him. Now he tossed it aside on the sofa in the first-class lounge where he and Laurian were waiting to board their flight.

'What on earth has cropped up that Jim Diss can't cope with, I wonder? Shan't be long.'

By this time Laurian knew they weren't flying east as she had anticipated, but westwards across the Atlantic. Their destination was Antigua, the island where, thirteen years ago, she had boarded the jumbo jet which had brought her to England.

It had been a shock to discover that Robert was taking her back to the Caribbean. For his sake, she had done her best to hide the fact that his carefully planned surprise had, at first, filled her with dismay.

Now that she had had time to adjust to it, while Robert scoured all the national newspapers for reports of last night's presentation, she was beginning to feel it might not be the ordeal it had seemed when he first broke it to her.

Robert didn't know about her childhood. It was something she had never discussed with anyone, not even with Jenny Lingfield and the boys, David and Neal, who had been respectively nineteen, seventeen and fourteen when she first met them. The baby, Susie, had been born after a long gap, when Barbara suddenly saw the menopause looming on the horizon and wanted to have one more child before it was too late.

When Robert came back from telephoning, she could tell before he reached her that whatever his secretary had wanted to tell him was serious. He was frowning and looking worried.

'What's happened?' she asked, as he sat down beside her, but only to perch on the edge of the sofa, not to sink back into his former relaxed posture.

'Nothing to do with the office. My sister's been on to them. Dad's had a heart attack. He's in intensive care and they think he'll pull through, but Mum wants me up there. I'm sorry, Laurie—I'll have to go.'

'Well, of course. We can rent a car and be there in a few hours.' She began to gather her things together, not sure now whether to be relieved or disappointed that her return to the West Indies was to be cancelled.

'No, no—you mustn't come. I want you to go ahead and I'll join you when I can. It might not be till next week, but you'll be all right on your own. They're nice hotels. You can swim and sunbathe . . . work up a nice tan.'

'I shouldn't dream of going without you. I can share the driving and, when we get there, I'm sure I can make myself useful . . . do the shopping . . . help with the cooking.'

'It's sweet of you, Laurie—but no. Your being there would only complicate things.'

'What do you mean?'

He took both her hands in his. 'I don't think you quite understand the kind of background I come from. My parents have a nice bungalow now, and a garden, but for years they lived in a little narrow terrace house with an outside w.c. and a bath which hung on a nail outside the back door, except on Friday nights when it stood on the living-room floor in front of the fire.'

'So? That's not unusual. The majority of people used to live like that and millions still do, I imagine. From what you've told me about her, I'm sure your mother never had a cockroach in her kitchen. I grew up with them running around all over the place.'

'You did?' Robert looked startled for a moment. Then, with only a short time left before boarding, he said hurriedly, 'I think you're exaggerating. You've got upper crust written all over you . . . certainly upper middle class. To put it in a nutshell, having someone from a posh background around—especially a famous designer—would only add to Mum's worries. She doesn't know about us—I haven't told her yet, and this isn't the right time. Please, Laurie—do as I ask you. Go on without me.'

'But Robert—'

'Don't argue with me. I want you to go. I loathe going home. I hate it. I don't belong there any more and I know, however worried she is about Dad, Mum will still have a moan about my marriage breaking up and never seeing her only grandchild. I'll be able to stand all that better if I know you're having the holiday I planned for you. Do it to please me . . . won't you?'

It was difficult to refuse the appeal in his eyes and in the pressure of his fingers as they squeezed hers. Laurian was beginning to realise that, just as she had kept certain things from him, he had glossed over his origins and the conflicting emotions he felt towards his parents. Clearly he was torn between a strong sense of duty towards them—no doubt it was he who had provided the bungalow and the garden—and a raging impatience with their narrower outlook.

'All right . . . I'll go,' she said doubtfully.

'Good girl! I'll give you your ticket. When I explain the situation, I'm sure they'll let me change mine. You'll also need the letters confirming our reservations. Everything's here in this wallet.' He handed her a plastic folder. 'I'll call you tonight.'

Ten minutes later, with Robert's farewell kiss still warm on her lips, she was installed in a comfortable seat in the first-class cabin, with a glass of sherry to sip while the aircraft taxied to the runway.

The flight took eight hours, but because of the time-change it was still daylight when they landed. Stepping from the air-conditioned cabin into the heat and humidity of a Caribbean afternoon, Laurian remembered waving to Archie from the door of the aircraft, and the tears which had poured down her cheeks as she peered through the porthole by her seat for a last glimpse of him among the crowd of West Indians who had come to wave goodbye to friends and relations who were returning to Britain or, like herself, venturing there for the first time.

If she had known it would be her last sight of her father ever, she would have run from the plane and refused to leave him.

When weekly letters stopped coming and she began to worry, the Lingfields had broken it to her that he had died. The cause of his death had been sudden heart failure, which Dr Lingfield had said was the best way to go when one's

time came. Heart failure . . . or heartbreak because he had
lost his island and his closest companion? There had been
no doubt in Laurian's mind of the answer to that. Secretly
she had sworn that, one day, she would get even with
Oliver, breaking *his* heart—if he had one.

That first white-hot desire for revenge had long since
cooled down and dissipated. But as Laurian sat in the taxi
taking her to the hotel Robert had chosen for their night-
stop, it was Oliver who occupied her thoughts.

During the flight she had discovered that the holiday
wasn't to be spent at the hotel in Antigua but, after another
short flight, at the Emerald Beach, the hotel not far from
the island Oliver had filched from them. For wasn't it,
morally, theft to buy something for almost nothing,
knowing it to be of great value? The smart alecs of the
world might consider such a deal fair pickings, but no
honourable person would.

Remembered sights, white egrets sitting on the backs of
scrawny cattle; a gang of small island boys with toothpaste
ad grins hopefully thumbing a lift from a passing beach
buggy driven by a lobster-pink tourist; two large laughing
women having a comfortable gossip on the steps of an iron-
roofed, strawberry pink wooden house, distracted her.

'You been to Antigua before, ma'am?' the driver
enquired.

'Yes, once . . . a long time age.' She leaned forward,
resting her arms on the back of the front passenger seat, and
began to ask him what had changed in the years since she
had left home.

Wearing a loose white T-shirt to protect her back and
shoulders from sunburn, her slim legs already the colour of
lightly done toast, Laurian skimmed across the breeze-

ruffled surface of the sea between the reef and the curve of white coral sand in front of the Emerald Beach hotel.

It had not taken long to recover her skill on a sailboard or to re-acclimatise to the heat which, most days, was moderated by the trade wind.

From where she stood, poised on her board, she could see the patch of deep water, tinged emerald green by the reflection of the jungle-like foliage growing on the headland above it, where *Euphrosyne* had lain at anchor. Beyond the headland, out of sight, was the island where she had been born. This afternoon, in a dinghy or one of the small cats provided for guests at the hotel, she was going to sail round the point to see what had become of her birthplace since Oliver got his hands on it.

Discreet enquiries among the Emerald Beach staff had revealed that the once nameless island, for long known as Bradford's Place, was now called the Palm Reef Club, owned by a Mr Thornham.

More information had come from a fellow guest, a plump, elderly blonde, with a fortune in rings on her fat little fingers, who had told Laurian last night that the place she had wanted to stay was at the Palm Reef.

'But they wrote that they didn't have a vacancy, and I don't believe that was true. I think they checked me out and didn't want me,' she had confided.

'Didn't want you, Mrs Lansing?'

'Well, you see, honey, I'm not "old money". Porter—that's my late husband—was the son of immigrants from Russia. I never met his folks, but I know they were very, very poor when they came to the States. The Palm Reef is very, very exclusive. You either have to have blue blood or be a State governor or a big star like Meryl Streep to stay there. I read in *Town & Country* that it's the most exclusive resort in the

Caribbean . . . a place where the top people know they'll only meet other top people, and where there's very tight security. I didn't really expect they would let me in, but it was worth a try.'

Although she had quickly adjusted to the heat, Laurian's body-clock was still making her sleepy by dinnertime and wakeful long before sunrise. This morning, reading in bed until it was light enough to go down to the deserted beach and watch the sky and sea flame with rose and gold lights as the fiery orb of the sun rose slowly above the horizon, she had known that she couldn't resist taking a look at the enclave of privilege and power Oliver Thornham had created.

It was curiosity which, the first night in Antigua, had made her change her mind about cancelling the Emerald Beach booking and staying where she was for two weeks. As he had promised he would, Robert had rung her to say his father was hanging on but was still on the danger list. Since then he had telephoned every night—late afternoon here—to report old Mr Adstock's progress.

'You sure do know how to handle that sailboard, Miss Ford,' said another of the American guests, when she brought it ashore.

Talking to Robert from Antigua, Laurian had told him she intended to register at the Emerald Beach as Ann Ford. He thought it was because she didn't want her real name to be recognised by any British guests. In fact it was to avoid the possibility that any of the staff here might connect her with Archibald Bradford, the last owner of the small island round the point.

'Thank you,' she said, smiling at the old man whose tanned paunch overhung the belt of his tartan Bermudas. 'It's mostly knack . . . like riding a bicycle. Once you know how, you never forget it.'

'Looks more than knack to me. Can I buy you a rum and Coke, Miss Ford?' He must have learned who she was from Mrs Lansing.

'A Coke on its own would be nice . . . and my first name is . . . Ann.' Telling a lie, even a white one, had never come easily to her.

'I'm Melvin Dorado. Call me Mel. Glad to know you, Ann. I'm from Cedar Rapids, Iowa.' As they walked up to the terrace together he began to tell her his life story.

Private Property. No admittance.

White lettering on a green board, the notice, one of several Laurian had seen, was clearly visible to anyone tempted to drop anchor near one of the small coves on the lee side of the island.

The warning failed to deter her from sailing close in to the shallows where she jumped over the side of the light fibreglass dinghy and made it fast before splashing ashore.

The island was greatly changed. She had seen that already. Where before, on this side, there had been only impenetrable vegetation, now each cove had a path leading to the other side of the island. Nature rampant was now nature couchant. And how! thought Laurian, discovering that the place where she had landed now had a shallow stone trough, containing tepid salt water, in which people could dabble their feet to remove the clinging white particles of coral.

In the bathrooms at the Emerald Beach there were notices requesting the guests to use similar footbaths because the pulverised coral forming the beach could clog the hotel's drains.

There, Laurian observed the request. Here, a profound resentment at the taming of her beloved wilderness made her ignore the trough. Barefoot, as of old, her slender feet slippered with specks of white, she set out along the path, wondering what Mrs Lansing had meant by 'very tight security'.

She wasn't left in doubt long. A few minutes later, acting on instinct, she turned and found someone following her; a big unsmiling West Indian in a white shirt with green epaulettes and the letters *PR* embroidered on the breast pocket.

'Good afternoon,' she said politely.

He advanced to within a yard of where she was standing. 'Can't you read, miss?' he asked, equally politely. 'This island is private. It tells you that back at the beach.'

He looked a tough cookie, she thought, and he didn't sound like an islander. His voice was brisker, with traces of an American accent. Perhaps, like herself, he belonged in the Caribbean but had spent a long time away.

'I see. I didn't notice. In that case I'll leave.' She turned back the way she had come, expecting him to step aside.

'I'm sorry, miss. You'll have to come with me.' He gestured for her to continue along the path.

'What for?' She saw now he was carrying a small walkie-talkie, such as London police used.

'All trespassers have to be checked out.'

'Look, I'm staying at the Emerald Beach. If you've seen how I got here, you'll have noticed it's one of their dinghies.'

'It's the rule. No exceptions. Go ahead, please.'

'Oh, really! How absurd,' Laurian protested. But, seeing it was useless to argue, she walked on towards the house.

The trees and shrubs thinned, giving place to a lawn kept green by sprinklers throwing bright veils of moisture in several directions. Beyond stood the house, almost unrecognisable with flowering creepers trained up its mellow stone walls, and the tall shutters painted white where before they had been a neglected, flaking blue-green.

'Turn left,' said the man behind her.

They skirted the lawn by a path leading in the direction of a one-storey extension which hadn't been there in her time. Casting swift glances around her, Laurian saw a great deal which was new. White loungers with pale blue cushions. Pavilions of dark green cotton, lined with flowery chintz, to shade groups of white wicker chairs. A steward in a spotless tunic taking a tray of long drinks to some people who were out of sight but whose voices and laughter could be heard.

Inside the extension, her escort moved ahead of her to tap on a door marked *Manager*. She heard someone say, 'Come in.' The security guard opened the door and nodded for her to enter.

The man behind the desk rose to his feet when she came in. Playing safe on the offchance that I might be someone important or know someone important, thought Laurian.

'Please sit down, Miss . . . ?'

'Ford.' She seated herself in the chair on the outer side of his large tidy desk.

'My name is Lynn.' He was a good-looking West Indian, aged around forty, dressed in a cream lightweight suit with a collar and tie. 'Why did you come ashore when it's clear this island is private, Miss Ford?'

Before she could answer, the door behind her opened and someone else looked in. A voice she recognised instantly said, 'John, I wonder if you would . . . oh, you're busy. Sorry to butt in. I'll come back later.'

The manager had again risen. There was a pause in which Laurian sat very still hoping her back view today—hair loose and wind blown, navy and white gingham shirt, khaki shorts, bare sandy feet—wouldn't ring any bells in the mind of the man in the doorway.

But it seemed that it did, because the door didn't close and

John Lynn said, 'This is Miss Ford who has just been caught trespassing, sir.'

Laurian didn't turn her head, but out of the corner of her eye she saw a tall form move into her range of vision and swing to face her. Her expression blank, she raised her eyes to Oliver Thornham's face and gave him a calm, level look which betrayed nothing of the turbulent feelings inside her.

If she had thought there was any possibility of meeting him, she would never have come. She had assumed—wrongly!— that he was still somewhere in Europe; and also that his ownership of the Palm Reef Club didn't necessarily mean he spent much of his time here.

He stared at her for several moments, taking in her somewhat dishevelled appearance from the blown-about shoulder-length hair to the coral clinging to her toes. As well as tanning her lightly, the sun had brought out reddish lights in her hair. For a tense moment she thought he was going to recognise her as the child who had turned away, scowling, when he held out his hand to say goodbye the day she had left here.

To her relief, he didn't. A slight and rather unpleasant smile touched the corners of his mouth.

'Miss Ford and I have met before, John. There's no need for you to waste your time with her. I'll deal with her myself.'

He returned to the door and opened it wide. 'This way, Miss Ford.'

They did not go far; only a short way down a corridor to another office which was empty. Oliver Thornham closed the door and indicated that she should sit down in the same place where she had sat in his manager's room. He himself didn't go behind the desk but leaned against the front of it, arms folded, feet crossed.

Unlike the spruce West Indian, he was more casually dressed in a white open-necked shirt and white shorts. He might have been going to play tennis—Laurian had heard the sound of ball hitting racquet as she passed the lawn—except that up to his knees his long brown legs were covered by white cotton stockings with neatly turned-down tops, worn with white bucksin loafers. Had they been lace-ups, and had his shirt sported blue and gold epaulettes, he would have looked like a Royal Navy officer about to deliver a homily to a member of the crew.

'As you know me, Mr Thornham, isn't this rather unnecessary? You can't seriously believe that I came here from any motive other than curiosity?' Laurian said coolly.

'But I don't know you, Miss Ford. I only know what you chose to tell me about yourself . . . and that you behaved very strangely the first time we met. I see no reason to take your word that you aren't one of the undesirables who bother us from time to time.'

She crossed her legs, showing her displeasure by drumming a devil's tattoo on the arm of the chair, the click of her nails on the wood indicating her impatience.

'What do you suspect me of? Wanting to assassinate someone staying here? Planning to steal your guests' jewels?'

'I agree that it seems unlikely, but we live in an age when such things do happen. Terrorists have frequently used attractive young women to smuggle arms and explosives. Guests in hotels do have their jewellery stolen if they're foolish enough to leave it in their rooms. It shouldn't take long to check you out. What's your first name, and where are you staying?'

'Ann Ford . . . the Emerald Beach.'

He uncrossed his ankles and swivelled to use one of the two telephones on the desk behind him. Evidently it was the house telephone. 'Get me the manager at Emerald Beach, would you, please?' Replacing the receiver, he looked at Laurian. 'When did you arrive, and how long are you staying?'

Mutinously, she told him.

'Are you alone?'

'Yes.'

The other telephone chirruped. He picked it up. 'Hello, Edgar. How are you? Good . . . yes, I'm fine, thanks. Got back last night. I'm a bit tied up for a few days, but I'll be over for a chat as soon as I'm free. Edgar, is there an Ann Ford staying with you? There is. The reason I ask is that I met her in London and probably ought to look her up while she's here. Depends if I can spare the time. Yes, you're right . . . she's a good-looking piece. Hoping to pick up one of the old goats, d'you think? No? Well, you're a good judge. You've seen plenty of gold-diggers in action. No, don't tell her I called in case I don't follow it up. See you soon. Goodbye.'

The call concluded, he returned his attention to Laurian. 'As you'll have gathered, my friend Edgar thinks you're an ornament to his hotel.'

'How flattering,' she said crisply. 'Now may I leave?'

'Not yet. That was only a preliminary enquiry which established that you are staying at Emerald Beach and, in Edgar's opinion, aren't on the prowl for a rich husband or protector. The next step is to speak to someone who can vouch that not only are you a bona fide holidaymaker but that you're an honest citizen who couldn't possibly have any sinister interest in the people who stay here. That shouldn't be difficult. If you were telling me the truth in London, I'll ring up whoever employs you as a designer.'

'I—I'm self-employed,' she told him.

'You mean you're a freelance?'

'No—I have a small business of my own.' By comparison

with the grand *haute couture* houses, *Laurian* was a small company.

'Then I'd better speak to your secretary or personal assistant.'

An old-fashioned nursery maxim flashed through Laurian's mind. *O, what a tangled web we weave, when first we practise to deceive.*

She said, 'I'm afraid that's not possible. She's on holiday as well—all my staff are. It's not unusual in the clothing trade. Whole factories close down for two weeks.'

'In August, yes. So I've heard. But at this time of year?' He looked sceptical.

'This time of year happens to be convenient for me and my employees.'

'All right . . . give me the name and number of one of your principal customers. There has to be someone who can vouch for you.'

For Laurian Bradford . . . not for Ann Ford, she thought. 'Look, Mr Thornham, it's expensive to call London . . . and totally unnecessary. Why not have your guard escort me back to my boat and I'll sail back to Emerald Beach and not come this way again. You have my word.'

'A word which may or may not be your bond,' he said drily. 'No, Miss Ford, you're not getting away with trespassing as easily as that. For one thing we happen to have someone very important arriving here tomorrow and I have to give his security people my word, which *is* my bond, that nothing untoward has happened recently. For another, I'm not too worried about causing you some annoyance. Your offensive behaviour in London—entirely gratuitous, as far as I could see—deserves some come-uppance, as my American guests say.'

He glanced at the watch on his strong wrist. 'There's

something which requires my attention, so I'm going to leave you here for fifteen minutes. That should give you plenty of time to think of someone who can guarantee your probity. I shall also expect a convincing explanation of your very strange volte-face when we had tea together.'

His expression cold and implacable, he went to the door, removed the key from the keyhole and went out, locking her in.

He's bluffing, Laurian thought. Paying me out for making him look a bit of an idiot in London. Trying to put the wind up me.

She bit her lip. And succeeding! she thought uneasily. He really had her on tenterhooks. Who did she know who would be so quick on the uptake that, when asked about Ann Ford, they would instantly twig that it was Laurian Bradford, for reasons best known to herself using a false name? The answer to that was—no one.

Nor was there any way to explain her behaviour at Fortnum's except by revealing her true identity and having the whole business out with him here and now. Which, for some reason, she didn't wish to do. Why, she wasn't quite sure, but all her instincts were against an immediate showdown.

Somehow, some way she was going to make certain that Oliver Thornham finally got *his* come-uppance for taking advantage of Archie thirteen years ago. But right at this moment she couldn't see how to achieve that.

Partly to give herself something to do, and partly because the scattering of coral offended her inherent sense of neatness, she looked around for a waste paper bin and began to pick up particles from the floor and then to remove those still adhering to her feet.

All the time she was brushing the bits off, some fragments of broken shell needing to be scraped off with her thumbnail, her brain was working like a mouse on a treadmill, scurrying frantically round and round but not getting anywhere. She remembered Archie sometimes using the French expression *un mauvais quart d'heure* when referring to various short-lived but unpleasant experiences in his life, starting with beatings at school. This was certainly one of the most uncomfortable quarters of an hour she had ever been through.

It was actually more than twenty minutes before the key turned in the lock and she braced herself for a second bout with him. But the person who entered the room was not her adversary but a pretty island girl in a white button-through overall with *PR* on the pocket.

'Would you come with me, please, ma'am.'

Laurian stood up. 'Where to?'

'To Mr Thornham's sittin' room, ma'am.'

A few minutes later she led Laurian from the new office extension into the house Archie had built. It brought a lump to her throat to cross the lofty hall to the stairs she had so often climbed on her way to sleep in an antique bed shrouded with fine mosquito netting.

The hall was no longer as she remembered it; neglected and shabby, with cobwebs in the corners of the ceiling and a film of dust on the great golden glass chandelier her father had bought in Venice in the Thirties.

Now beautiful Persian rugs were spread about on the flagstones and two gorgeous bursts of hibiscus stood on giltwood torchères on either side of the tall double doors giving on to the veranda. They were open and through them she could see two men, both of whose faces she had seen in *Time* magazine recently, and two women, presumably their wives, being served with afternoon tea.

As she followed the maid up the broad sweep of the

staircase, a middle-aged woman, exuding elegance in spite of being dressed in a man's shirt worn loose over white Bermudas, came drifting leisurely down. She smiled. Laurian smiled back. It wasn't until moments later that she realised she had just passed an actress who had been a great star for forty years but was now never seen in public. She looked fifty-something but must be at least sixty-five.

At the top of the stairs, a wide corridor ran the length of the house with a Venetian window at either end and doors all along both sides. The maid led the way to the seaward door at the south end. She was about to knock when it opened and an attractive woman in a sun-dress appeared. Even though she was on edge, Laurian noticed the dress was made from an unusual and pleasing print.

The woman smiled at them both and went on her way. The maid waited for Laurian to enter the room and then closed the door.

'Come through to the balcony, Miss Ford,' said Oliver Thornham, who was standing on the threshold of the French windows.

She had a fleeting impression of a comfortably furnished sitting-room, one wall lined with recently published books in colourful wrappers, and another covered with paintings of sailing ships, before she emerged on to the balcony where a table was set for tea, except that in place of a teapot there was a glass pitcher of iced coffee.

'Mary Poole, whom you passed on your way in, runs our shop,' he told her, with a gesture inviting her to take one of the two cushioned chairs facing the sea.

As she did so, she noticed that the balcony, once a long open space set about with creaking cane loungers and weather beaten directors' chairs, had been divided into smaller balconies, the partitions between them overhung by the same vivid bougainvillaeas and flowering vines which made the new parts of the building blend with the main house.

'May I offer you some of this?' he asked, lifting the pitcher.

'Even though I might be a sneak thief or something worse?' she asked, with a trace of sarcasm.

He began to fill one of the two tall glasses. 'I think it's unlikely, but I can't afford to take chances. Have you decided who you want me to call?'

Coming along the corridor, Laurin had decided to call his bluff.

'No, I haven't.'

He gave her a thoughtful look. 'Try one of these. They're a speciality of the house. I wonder if you'll know what the filling is.' He offered her a plate of thin brown bread sandwiches.

Laurian sipped some iced coffee which was made with cream and liberally laced with brandy. When she bit into a sandwich, she knew instantly that it contained Gentleman's Relish, which Archie had used to have sent from Harrods in white glass pots, one of his last surviving extravagances.

'Cucumber and something else. Whatever it is, it's a very good combination.'

'We think so. The something else is Patum Peperium, a rather old-fashioned paste more usually spread on hot toast.'

He didn't say who had introduced him to it; although it was possible he had eaten the paste as a schoolboy in England.

Curious to hear what he told people about his connection with the house, she asked, 'Were you born in this part of the world? Did this house belong to your family?'

The sound of laughter from the beach below made Oliver turn his head and gave her a view of his strongly drawn, rather fierce profile.

Watching a young man pursue a girl through the shining shallows, he said, 'No, I only came here about a dozen years ago. The house was built by a somewhat eccentric Englishman whose fortunes had gradually declined. At one time, I believe, it was the scene of wonderful house-parties. Everyone who was anyone came here, but only if they were amusing or interesting or, in the case of women, beautiful. I've tried to recapture that atmosphere, and I think I've succeeded.'

'And made *your* fortune in the process, I imagine,' said Laurian, in a carefully expressionless voice.

His answer to that was, 'Everyone concerned has benefited. I have the best staff in this part of the Caribbean because I pay the highest wages and provide the best living conditions. As far as possible, everything we use is made or grown locally. We make substantial contributions towards improviding the amenities on the big island. I don't mean amenities for tourists but for islanders. For instance, there are several Palm Reef scholarships to help young people go to America or Britain for specialised training.'

'You make yourself sound more like a philanthropist than a business man,' she said dryly.

'I believe it's possible to be both. Certainly for someone like myself who has neither a board nor shareholders to insist on excessive profits, and whose personal needs are fairly modest.'

Was he speaking the truth? Or was this a 'line'? she wondered. If it were the truth, his views must have changed. They didn't tie in with the price he had paid for the island in the first place.

She rose and moved to the balustrade, one hand holding the cold glass, the other resting on the warm stone which would hold the heat of the day long after the brief tropical dusk had changed the sky from blue to black and signalled innumerable cicadas to begin their after-dark chorus.

Oliver rose and came to stand alongside but not close to her. 'How do you like the Caribbean? Has it come up to your expectations?'

'Antigua looked rather arid, but these two islands are beautiful.'

'Do you think, if you'd been born here, you would have wanted to leave?' he asked.

What a question for him to ask her! She was tempted to re-open hostilities which at least on his side, she gathered, were undergoing a cease-fire while refreshments were in progress.

'I should think, for anyone born here, having to leave all this would almost break their hearts.'

'I think so too,' he agreed. 'No one in their right mind would voluntarily go away. They would have to be driven by poverty, lack of work and so on. People were forced to emigrate because there was little or no opportunity to improve their conditions here; not because they wanted to live in large cities and wear overcoats half the year. If, in the last century and earlier, businessmen hadn't thought only of profits and had tried to found a more balanced economy here, there would never have been the great exodus of recent times with all its difficult consequences.'

He turned sideways, hitching one long thigh on to the wide top of the balustrade, facing her. 'I'm afraid that's one of my hobby horses, the other being conservation.' He gestured towards the line of breakers marking the hidden barrier of coral between the lagoon and the deep sea. 'We're trying not to kill off our reef as has happened round other islands. People don't realise that washing powders, bath gels, cleaning agents—all the chemical gunk we take for granted nowadays— is poison to other living things.'

If I hadn't known anything about him, if we had just met for the first time, I should have liked him, thought Laurian. But they had met before, and it had been his cupidity which had caused her own unwilling exile. That it had turned out well eventually didn't make him less blameworthy. The end never justified the means if they were wrong and cruel.

She drained the last of the potent coffee. Perhaps it was rum, not brandy, which gave it its kick. She looked at her watch. 'I borrowed the dinghy for two hours. If I don't start back soon, they'll think something has happened and come looking for me.'

'Do I take it you've changed your mind now? What's the number you want me to ring?'

She lifted her chin and her topaz eyes flashed impatiently. 'This nonsense has gone on long enough. I'm not going to give you a number. I'm not going to be "checked out". You've already kept me locked in for twenty minutes. Enough is enough, Mr Thornham.'

He shrugged and gave a resigned sigh. 'That isn't a helpful attitude. It suggests you have something to hide. I'm afraid I'm going to have to detain you until you feel more co-operative.' He stood up and circled the tea-table, saying more briskly, 'I'll have the dinghy towed back with a message that you're staying for dinner and the launch will bring you back later. That is, of course, if by then you've seen reason. If not, you'll be here overnight.'

'Overnight!' Laurian exclaimed, aghast. 'You can't . . . You've no right to keep me!'

He swung round, the same grim expression she had seen before he locked the door hardening his features again.

'You don't seem to understand the situation, Miss Ford. Here I have any rights I choose to exert. I'm a patient man and, while my patience lasts, you won't find being held here unpleasant. But I must warn you it won't last for ever. If you persist in being difficult, I may have to take sterner measures.'

Leaving her to conjecture what they might be, he strode through his sitting-room and disappeared into the corridor.

CHAPTER THREE

FOR SOME MOMENTS after he had gone, Laurian stood very still, holding her temper in check. A strong desire to stamp, swear and throw things had swept over her as Oliver left the adjoining room; impulses she never felt normally.

Hers was not an inflammable nature. She hadn't been angry for years. In fact, now she came to think of it, the last time she had lost her temper was the day she had swum to *Euphrosyne* and upbraided Oliver for brainwashing Archie into thinking he had to send her to England.

Mastering her rage at his high-handed attitude, she picked up another sandwich. Several days of outdoor living and almost continuous exercise had sharpened her appetite. The half-forgotten taste of the Gentleman's Relish, which she had never had in England, was a strong reminder of Archie. Suddenly, even though the balcony had been changed since they used to sit there, she felt his presence very strongly. It calmed and comforted her. Her father had been in innumerable tight spots during his long life.

During the Second World War, a very fit man only a few years older than Oliver was now, and speaking fluent modern Greek, he had been parachuted into Greece to take charge of a daring guerrilla operation. 'Keep calm' had been his watchword. Remembering that, Laurian took another sandwich and made herself stroll leisurely into the sitting-room to have a look round it.

No one could ever have mistaken it for anything but a man's

room. There was nothing 'pretty' about the décor, and none of the treasured bits and pieces which Laurian herself had accumulated on forays to a Mayfair antiques market not far from her showroom. The several hundred books on the shelves and in overflow stacks around the room seemed to cover a wide range of subjects. Everything from *haute cuisine* to survival techniques and philosophy.

The lower shelves had been made deeper to accommodate a set of encyclopaedias and other large heavy volumes. Where the top of these shelves formed a ledge stood a number of framed photographs. There was one of a Naval officer and his bride, the style of her dress and veil suggesting a date in the late Forties. The couple were obviously Oliver's parents. There were other informal pictures of them in later years, and one of his father as an elderly man, white-haired, with a sombre expression, perhaps because by then he was a widower.

There was also an enlarged rather grainy snapshot of Oliver and a girl. They were sitting in the cockpit of a boat, wearing guernseys, grinning at the photographer. His sister? He had never spoken of his family after he came to the island and Archie had made a point of never asking strangers about themselves until they started to volunteer information. Oliver never had.

The most unexpected thing in the room, sitting at the end of the ledge, was a worn, one-eyed teddy bear wearing a red knitted waistcoat fastened by two red-topped toadstool buttons.

Laurian knew several women who still had their childhood bed-partners, and she had heard of men, such as the late Sir John Betjeman, who had life-long attachments to their bears. She wouldn't have thought Oliver Thornham capable of such sentimental feeling.

'Miss Ford? I'm Mary Poole. I run the hotel shop.'

As Laurian swung round from her puzzled contemplation of the threadbare stuffed animal with his single boot-button eye, the woman she had seen earlier advanced into the room to shake hands.

'How do you do.'

As they smiled at each other, Laurian knew that here was someone she could like. Somewhere between Oliver and herself in age, Mary Poole gave an immediate impression of being warm-hearted, sensible and gentle. She wore her hair in a chin-length streaky-blonde bob and Laurian guessed that she had her eyelashes dyed—they were dark but not mascaraed—and that she put nothing on her face but sun-protection cream and lipstick. Since arriving in the Caribbean, this had been her own routine except that, being naturally dark, her lashes didn't need dyeing.

'Oliver tells me you're a fashion designer. Would it interest you to come and look round the shop?' the other woman asked.

'Very much . . . thank you.' Laurian wondered what else Oliver had said about her.

On the way downstairs, she noticed that Mary Poole was wearing a wedding ring and wondered if her husband was also employed here.

If Mrs Poole had been deputed to find out if Laurian was what she claimed to be, she was too intelligent to start probing straight away. Instead she talked about the problem of finding things to appeal to the women who stayed at the Club; women accustomed to shopping in New York, Toronto and London.

After Laurian had spent some time admiring the hand-printed cotton voile shirts cut loosely to be worn as cool cover-ups, and other resort wear run up by seamstresses on the big island, two customers entered the shop which was in one of the downstairs rooms.

Judging that the newcomers were in a spending mood, Laurian said, 'I'll come back later.'

'Yes, do.' Mary—she had asked to be called that—showed no sign of being fussed about letting Laurian out of her sight.

Not that there's much, if any, chance of my escaping, she thought, leaving the shop by the door giving on to the veranda. It wouldn't have been impossible for her to swim back to her hotel. She knew that, if put to it by, say, a shipwreck, she could swim for several miles.

It was getting into the water which was the problem. She didn't think it had been by chance that the guard with the walkie-talkie had caught her so quickly. It was her belief that the grounds of the Palm Reef Club were under surveillance by hidden cameras, and somewhere in the club buildings one or more monitor screens were showing what was happening at all the approaches to the island. If she was right, there had been no need for Oliver to lock her in earlier. If she did attempt to get away by swimming, she would be seen and intercepted by a power-boat.

The assurance that no outsiders could infiltrate their exclusive hideaway might please most of the people who came to the re-styled Bradford's Place, but it made Bradford's daughter feel as if she were in a luxurious detention centre.

She was wondering what Archie would make of the present set-up when her eye was caught by yet another thing which hadn't been here in their time; a carved limetone plaque in the style of those seen on the walls of old churches. This one was attached to the wall at the back of the veranda, close to the double doors of the hall where no one entering the house could fail to see it.

Incised in the stone, in clear Roman lettering, was Archie's name, followed by his decorations, and the dates of his birth and death. Below this was recorded the year in which the foundations had been laid of 'this fine house which he designed incorporating certain features of his family seat, Kingscote Abbey, England'.

But it was what followed this which Laurian found the most moving, and which she read through a shimmer of tears.

Here, after many adventures, he found quietude, peace and beauty which he shared with his many friends and with more than one stranger.
Life is mostly froth and bubble,
Two things stand like stone,
Kindness in another's trouble,
Courage in one's own.
Here lived a man who had kindness and courage in full measure.

She was still gazing at it, but had had time to blink away her tears, when from behind her Oliver said, 'That memorial tablet was the last work of an old West Indian stone carver who had worked for Mr Bradford when the house was going up. Let me show you round.'

Not wanting him to guess the effect the inscription had had on her, she said with delicate sarcasm, 'Is that wise? I might make mental notes to pass on to my partners in crime.'

'You might. I don't think you will. I've just been speaking to Mary. She likes you, and she's a good judge of people. Her opinion confirms what I think—that you came ashore out of curiosity.'

'Then why not let me go?'

'Because you refuse to prove your *bona fides.*'

'Did you tell Mrs Poole why you were keeping me prisoner?'

'No: she thinks I met you in Europe—which is true—and

you're here at my invitation. Only John Lynn, my manager, and one of the guards know the truth.'

'And the maid who unlocked the office where you left me,' Laurian reminded him.

'Oh, yes . . . Louise. She won't spread that around. All the staff here are very discreet.'

I'm sure they are. If you hold outsiders against their will, what would you do to someone on your payroll who transgressed? Chain them below the tideline like pirates, I shouldn't wonder.' She spoke flippantly but with the underlying conviction that he might pay high wages but he would make life extremely unpleasant for anyone who failed to come up to his exacting standards.

'Something like that. This way.' He touched her elbow with his fingers to steer her from the veranda to the terrace between the house and the beach. It was the lightest, most impersonal of physical contacts, much less intimate than shaking hands, yet it sent a tingle up her arm and was an unwelcome reminder of the attraction she had felt before she discovered who he was.

'What size shoes do you take?'

The question was so unexpected that she answered, 'Five,' automatically.

'Excuse me a moment. I'll be right back.'

Standing where he had left her, she guessed he had gone to fetch something for her to put on her feet. Although she had done it all her life, up to the age of thirteen, and had come to no harm, guests at the Emerald Beach were advised against going barefoot except on the beach. There were small tick-like creatures to be found in the grass which could penetrate visitors' soft soles and set up infections.

When Oliver returned, he was carrying a pair of the canvas slippers she had seen in Mary's shop.

'I think these should fit you. Sit down.' He indicated the low stone parapet which prevented the sand from invading the terrace.

Laurian sat, but when she put out her hand to take the espadrilles from him, he went down on his haunches and took hold of one of her ankles to put them on for her.

To distract herself from the tremor running up her leg, she said hurriedly, 'These must be French. I believe they're the only ones which are reinforced at the toe with that special stitching.'

'They are French. Mary has a contact in Martinique who imports them from France and supplies her. Stand up to make sure it fits.'

She obeyed him. 'It's fine . . . but I haven't any money with me to pay for them.'

'We'll put it on your bill.'

When she sat down he lifted her other foot, pausing before putting on the second espadrille to say, 'You have beautiful feet. These have never been squashed into tight shoes.' His palm moved from the back of her ankle to cup her smooth heel.

Laurian swallowed to clear a constriction in her throat. 'I've always done as men do and worn comfortable shoes with low heels. The only time I wear high heels is when I'm going to a party and won't have to walk any distance. I hate seeing women teetering about the street on three-inch stilettos. That isn't being feminine. It's being stupid.'

Oliver was still holding her heel in one hand and the beige espadrille in the other. Beige, navy, black and white were the only colours Mary stocked. He seemed to be studying Laurian's toe, making her glad she had had a professional pedicure before coming on holiday, and only that morning had re-painted her toenails with the same colourless varnish she used on her fingernails.

'I agree.' He looked into her eyes. 'But women's idea of glamour and what men think attractive doesn't always correspond. When you walked from Hatchards to Fortnum's ahead of me the other day, I thought you were probably one of the few well-dressed women in London whose feet weren't killing her. Of course you have the advantage of being tall and having good legs.'

She had never thought of her heels as erogenous zones, but there was no denying her reaction to Oliver's touch. It gave her a strange, mad desire to reach out and plunge her fingers into his thick dark hair.

Ignoring the compliment, she said, 'You mentioned my bill. Don't tell me you'll have the gall to charge me for keeping me here under duress?'

He fitted the rope-soled shoe on to her foot and, with one lithe movement, rose from his crouching position. His height emphasised by the fact that she was still sitting while he stood, he looked down at her with an expresion she couldn't read.

'Certainly—and perhaps I should warn you that our rates are considerably higher than those at Emerald Beach. With, of course, the usual supplement for single occupancy.'

Was he serious? Or making fun of her? It was impossible to tell.

'If the expense worries you, the remedy is in your hands,' he added smoothly.

At that moment a steward came to tell him he was wanted on the telephone. Oliver said, 'Excuse me,' and walked away.

Even though she was fuming again, Laurian couldn't help thinking he had very good legs himself. As he strode across the terrace, her eyes followed him, travelling upwards from his shapely white-stockinged ankles, past the swell of his calves to the lightly furred backs of his brown thighs and the hard male backside outlined by his well-cut shorts. As she looked at those muscular buttocks and, above them, the long back broadening to wide powerful shoulders, thoughts of what it would be like to be held by him, kissed by him, sent a long shiver through her.

She found it confusing and disturbing to be attracted physically to a man she disliked and distrusted intellectually. And yet, to give the devil his due, he had put up the plaque commemorating her father and paying tribute to Archie's qualities. That was unexpectedly nice of him. She would have thought Oliver would have preferred to forget the old man and the child who had been here when he arrived. Clearly the child was forgotten. Even dressed as she was now, with her hair in a breeze-whipped tangle, he had not seen any resemblance to the skinny little thing who had once hero-worshipped him.

In case the telephone call involved him in more pressing matters than showing her round what was now his domain, she decided not to wait for him to come back.

As she left the terrace and strolled in the direction of what, long ago, had been a favourite place to lie reading, she pondered again the seriousness of his threat to charge her for staying here if she continued to hold out against his insistence on verifying her identity.

Why *was* she holding out? It would be so much simpler to reveal who she really was. But then she would also have to accuse him of doing Archie down over the sale of the island, and she still wasn't ready for that confrontation. For a while longer she wanted to observe him from behind the screen of her assumed name.

The hammock slung between two palm trees at the edge of the beach was still there. Not the same discoloured canvas hammock in which, as a child, she had lain reading *Moby Dick* and P.G. Wodehouse and Baroness Orczy, but a brightly coloured woven grass double hammock, piled with vivid cotton cushions, in which a woman in a sleek black one-piece and a white cotton sun-hat was flipping through *Harpers & Queen*.

She glanced up as Laurian passed by and then gave a cry of surprise.

'Laurian! I almost didn't recognise you. When did you arrive? I thought you'd be in London, basking in your latest success. Congratulations. I read that you'd carried off the Fashion Council's award in Henry's *Times* the next day.'

Lady Henry Buckland, wife of the younger son of the Duke of Bromsgrove, had been one of Laurian's best customers for several years and also, with her striking if rather brittle blonde looks, an excellent advertisement.

'Hello, Lady Henry. I didn't recognise you either.' It came to Laurian that this glamorous aristocrat with whom, if not actually friendly, she had long been on easy terms, was the very person she needed to help her out of her fix. 'I'm not staying here. Actually I'm trespassing.'

Quickly, she explained the situation. 'I have a particular reason for not wanting anyone here to know who I am for the time being.'

'How intriguing,' said Lady Henry. 'Could it be that you're related to the old boy who built the house . . . Archibald Bradford?' she asked shrewdly. 'His granddaughter, perhaps?'

'If you don't mind, I'd rather not go into that at the moment. But you have my word that there's nothing fishy going on. If you would be kind enough to vouch for me, it won't involve you in anything you wouldn't like.'

'I'm sure it won't. Of course I'll vouch for you. Who is this VIP who's due to arrive soon, I wonder? We've been here two days and I must say it's rather bliss not to have any Ghastlies around. I don't know how the management here is able to keep them at bay—most of the larger islands are swarming with terrible people—but so far we haven't seen anyone we want to avoid. Where are you staying if not here?'

Laurian told her and, when asked, had to admit that her fellow guests at Emerald Beach did include several people whom Lady Henry would consider Ghastlies.

'What a bore for you,' said the other woman. 'Can't you move here, or are they full up?'

'I don't know, but I'm quite happy where I am. I spend most of the time sailing and windsurfing.'

'How energetic! All I want to do is loll. My husband is somewhere out there . . . snorkeling up and down the reef with two or three other enthusiasts. I only see him at meals and in the evening. I don't mind. It amuses him and if I get bored there's an air-conditioned gym and one can also have beauty treatments. What are the men like at your place? Anyone interesting?'

Laurian shook her head. She knew that Lady Henry was reputed to have a roving eye and wondered if it had roved in Oliver's direction, or if she wouldn't consider the owner of an hotel—even of an exceptionally exclusive hotel—a suitable partner in dalliance.

'There's only one here,' said Lady Henry. 'But he doesn't mingle much. He seems to have most of his meals in private. Perhaps he's a writer, working on a book or something. Does the name Thornham ring any bells with you?'

'The man who owns the Club is called Thornham. Oliver Thornham. Tall . . . dark . . .'

'. . . and extremely attractive,' Lady Henry remarked, with a gleam in her blue eyes. 'Do you know him?'

'He's the person I want you to vouch for me to.'

'I see. I thought you meant it was the manager—Lynn, I

think his name is—who was worried you might be up to no good. If it's the dark man, let's go and find him at once.'

She tipped herself out of the hammock, swathed herself in a diaphanous black and white kanga and stepped into leather mules. 'Wait a moment, I must have a quick touch-up.'

Watching her paint her mouth, Laurian was disconcerted by Lady Henry's undisguised eagerness to meet Oliver. Not that it should surprise her. He was the kind of man at whom any woman, married or single, ripe for a holiday affair, would look hungrily. She wondered if he took the opportunities offered him.

He had told her in Fortnum's restaurant that he wasn't married, had never been married and didn't have an unofficial partner. But he was too fit and virile-looking to be a celibate. She was conscious of mentally shrinking from the idea that he might be promiscuous; amusing himself with women like Lady Henry whose husbands didn't satisfy them or who enjoyed the element of danger in illicit sex.

'You had better call me Atalanta if we're supposed to be friends,' said the other woman, peering at he reflection in a hand mirror taken from her beach bag.

'I've mentioned that I'm a designer to him. I think it would be best to stick to the truth and say I've designed clothes for you.'

'It's not impossible that someone else here may know you . . . by name and sight, if not personally,' Lady Henry pointed out, as they walked towards the house. 'Have you thought of that?'

'Designers have to be very famous for a long time to be widely recognised,' said Laurian. 'The chances of another of my customers being here while I am is fairly remote, I think.'

'I'm dying to know what's behind all this. You will tell me eventually, I hope?'

Laurian was saved from having to promise she would by the sight of Oliver walking towards them.

As he came within speaking distance, she said, 'I've met someone who will allay your doubts about me, Mr Thornham. Lady Henry, may I introduce Oliver Thornham who owns this island?'

'How do you do?' Lady Henry gave him her hand. 'I do envy you, living in this divine spot all the year round. I so loathe English winters. Ann tells me you suspect her of being up to no good because she sneaked ashore without permission. I can assure you she's absolutely respectable. Half the clothes in my wardrobe are her designs.'

Her hand still in his—who was prolonging the contact it was impossible for Laurian to tell—Oliver said, 'How do you do, Lady Henry? I'm glad you like Palm Reef. It's your first visit here, I believe? I hope you'll enjoy it enough to want to become an *habituée*.' He looked at Laurian. 'In that case your "duress" is over, Miss Ford. Perhaps you'll think twice about ignoring *No Admittance* signs in future. I'm afraid I can't have you taken back to your hotel immediately. All our boats are in use at present.'

'Why not stay and have dinner with us, Ann?' Atalanta suggested. 'And why don't you join us, Oliver, and make amends for your nasty suspicions about her?'—this with a melting look which made it clear it wasn't Laurian she expected him to chat up.

'Thank you, I'd like to,' he said, with alacrity.

Adjoining Mary Poole's boutique was her private lavatory and shower where, before joining the others for dinner that night, Laurian washed herself and her hair and used one of the dryers kept by the housekeeper for guests who had forgotten to pack their own.

By this time Mary had gone home to the larger island where she had a small house left to her by her parents who had retired there. After her father's death, her mother, who had never felt comfortable living overseas, had returned to England to live with her sister in a flat in Bournemouth. Mary, widowed when her husband was killed on Army service in Northern Ireland, had taken over the house. She had no children. These details of her circumstances had emerged during a conversation while Laurian was choosing something to wear; dinner at the Club being black tie every night, she had discovered.

The dress she had bought was made of batik-printed cotton voile in shades of amber with splashes of dark red. It was cut on the lines of a poncho with a hole for her neck and slits for her arms to pass through. The lining was another circle of plain amber voile attached to the binding of the neck but hemmed independently. Under this Laurian wore the fudge-coloured bikini she had had on under her shirt and shorts. With the light behind it, the dress showed the outlines of her body. It was intended to.

The shop had also supplied a necklet of dyed-red seeds with ear-rings to match which Mary had found while hunting for stock in Trinidad. The Club's beauty shop had provided a lipstick and eye-shadow, and Atalanta Buckland, who took the same size shoes, had offered to lend Laurian bronze kid sandals.

So it was with a satisfactory feeling of looking not her best but presentable enough to pass muster in a gathering of the *crème de la crème* from both sides of the Atlantic that she set out from the boutique to find her companions for the evening.

Atalanta and her husband were having drinks on the now lantern-lit terrace, but Oliver wasn't with them when Laurian's approach and a murmur from his wife brought

Henry Buckland to his feet.

He came as a surprise to Laurian. She had expected him to be either dull, asinine or hearty, or a combination of all three. In fact he wasn't bad looking in a high-coloured English way, and he soon showed himself to be jolly and even rather witty. She couldn't imagine why Atalanta needed to flirt with other men when she had such an affable husband. But perhaps there was more, or less, to their marriage than met the eye.

'Are you a snorkeler, Ann?' he asked presently.

'I have snorkeled—yes. You're very keen on it, I hear.'

'Tremendously keen,' he agreed, his eyes lighting with enthusiasm. 'I first tried it in the Pacific when Atalanta and I were honeymooning in Fiji. I wasn't frightfully taken with Fiji, actually. Neither of us were, were we, darling?'

'Ghastly place,' said Atalanta, with a grimace. 'The *last* place to go for a honeymoon. Swelteringly hot and seething with mosquitoes. I can't think what made us choose it. It was a total disaster.'

'Not *total,* darling—no, no. The big island wasn't much to write home about, but that chain of smaller islands was absolutely first rate.' Henry turned to Laurian. 'If you ever want an out-of-this-world experience, go on the Blue Lagoon cruise through the Yasawa group. Quite unforgettable! About thirty or forty people on a smallish boat with a Fijian captain and crew. It only lasts for three days, but the swimming and snorkeling are superb. Even better than here, as a matter of fact. The snag is, of course, that it takes so damned long to fly out there. This place is far more accessible.'

'And far more civilised,' was his wife's emphatic comment. 'Talking of Ghastlies,' she said to Laurian,' some of the people on that cruise were the absolute end!' She paused. 'But the crew were rather gorgeous. *Huge* men wearing wraparound skirts, which somehow made them doubly macho, and often a frangipani flower stuck in their frizzy black hair.'

A reminiscent glint in her eyes made Laurian wonder if, while Henry was exploring the wonders beneath the sea, Atalanta had had her first post-marital frolic with a giant Fijian.

'Were the fish and the corals quite different from those you've seen here?' she asked him.

This launched Henry on a detailed comparison of submarine life in the Pacific and the Caribbean, a discourse to which Laurian, who had once been something of an expert on the latter, listened with interest.

At the same time she was aware that Atalanta was bored, perhaps not unreasonably. To someone who didn't snorkel, descriptions of fish were as tedious as verbal re-plays of games of golf or bridge. Having snorkeled happily all day, Henry would have been wise to concentrate on his wife and her interests during the evening, thought Laurian, with a twinge of guilt for having given him the cue for this detailed account of his day's advanture.

It was cut short by the arrival of Oliver, looking even broader of shoulder in a white dinner jacket which also emphasised the darkness of his skin. The light from the strings of crimson Japanese lanterns and the candles burning inside the cranberry glass storm shields gave a Red Indian tinge to his bronzed skin; and the upward play of light on his face as Atalanta introduced her husband, and the two men shook hands, threw into sharper relief the forceful modelling of his chin, the thrust of the aquiline nose and the jut of his eyebrows above the piercing grey eyes. With longer hair and a headcloth, he could have posed for a painting of Geronimo or some other great chief.

However, it was only his facial features which had a certain wildness about them, a suggestion of something untamed in the spirit of the man within. His general appearance couldn't have been more civilised or his manners more urbane as he complimented Atalanta on her dress.

'Is that one of Ann's designs?' he asked.

'No, this is American . . . Calvin Klein. Ann knows I'm not faithful to her if something irresistible by another designer comes my way.'

Was she telling him something else: that she wasn't faithful to her husband if an irresistible man came her way? Laurian wondered. She glanced at Henry. He was taking another rum punch from a tray offered by a steward and didn't appear to have heard his wife's remark.

'Their skills may not compare with your own, but that dress by one of our local designers looks very good on you,' Oliver told Laurian.

'Thank you.'

She sensed that his approval was merely a counterbalance to his tribute to Atalanta; a practised compliment from the owner of the Palm Reef Club rather than from the man behind the suave public persona.

In the shadows at the end of the terrace, a small steel band was playing soft background music. She recognised the theme from the movie *Out Of Africa* and asked Henry if he had seen it. They all had. A discussion of the film, the stars and the book on which it had been based kept the conversation going until they moved to the open-air dining-room which was another addition to the original building.

By now the moon had risen and was silvering the sea which lapped gently against the blanched beach within yards of the Bucklands' table.

'How did you come to own the island, Oliver?' asked Atalanta, when they had finished deciding what to eat. 'Are you a kinsman of Archibald Bradford?'

'No, I bought it from him. I was on a voyage which should have been made with the girl I was going to marry. The original plan was to sail to New Zealand, which we both liked the sound of. Then Judy was drowned in a gale off the south coast of England. For something to do, I started out alone, intending to sail round the world. This was as far as I got . . . rather like the family who started the restoration of English Harbour in Antigua. They were bound for Australia, so the story goes, until they came on the remains of the naval docks there and were fired with the idea of saving them from complete dereliction. In the same way, I saw the possibilities of reviving this place. It was in a pretty bad way when I first saw it.'

Judy. Laurian remembered a day when she had sat beside him as he lay asleep on the beach and had heard him mutter that name followed by 'darling'. He must have been dreaming of the girl he had loved, whom the sea had taken. What a horrible let-down to find it wasn't Judy standing beside him but a child too young to know about passion or frustration.

'How terribly sad . . . losing your future wife,' said Atalanta sympathetically. 'And you've never met anyone else you wanted to marry?'

'For a long time after that I couldn't afford a wife. I had to sell my boat to raise the money to buy the island. The price wasn't high considering the potential of the place, but it stretched my resources to their limit,' Oliver replied. 'For several years afterwards, it was touch and go whether my aims would be realised.'

'But now I should think you could afford to support a whole harem of wives,' said Atalanta. 'Can't you find even one to suit you? Or do you prefer to play the field?'—with one of her sexy looks.

To Laurian's surprise, he said, 'I was never inclined to play the field even as a young man, Lady Henry.'

This reversion to formality after she had told him to use her first name seemed to Laurian a rather marked set-down. Considering how the other woman had helped her out of spot, it was unworthy to feel pleased that she had been put in her place, but Laurian couldn't help it.

For the first time she began to think she might have musjudged Oliver . . . jumped to conclusions about him which were not well founded.

If Atalanta recognised the rebuff, she wasn't quashed by it. She eyed him with an impish expression, as if she liked a man who didn't succumb to her charms too readily.

Henry seemed unaware of these nuances. He had listened to Oliver's account of how he had come to the island, but now he was having another glance at the wine list. Evidently wine was one of his interests. He began to enquire into the problems of importing wines from Europe and storing them in a hot climate.

This was a subject his wife found as boring as snorkeling. Her eyes wandered round the dining-room, appraising the other women's clothes. Laurian began to wonder what did interest Atalanta, apart from clothes and gossip. Her own interest in wine had been developed by Archie, who had held that the perfect breakfast was a peach and a glass of Riesling and the best aid to a sound night's sleep a glass of vintage port and a handful of walnuts. However, although she could have contributed opinions on European wines, she didn't, and when the talk turned to American wines she kept silent from lack of knowledge and a wish to learn.

Many men would have thought it natural for women to hold their tongues when a subject which was, by tradition, a male preserve was under discussion.

As the first course was removed and the second brought to

them, Atalanta made a remark about the absence of mosquitoes on the island. While Henry was agreeing with her, Oliver turned to Laurian.

'You're very quiet, Ann. Are you tired? Was finding yourself under restraint such an ordeal?'

It was said in a tone of gentle raillery which at once took her back to the days when she had welcomed his presence, before he had killed all her warm, loving feelings towards him by being the author of her exile.

'Not at all. It's only that I'm . . . dazed by this lovely place. Don't you ever wish you didn't have to share it with other people . . . that you could have it all to yourself?'

'To do that I should have to be a millionaire . . . *not* one of my objects in life,' he said drily.

'What are your objects?'

'To live well in pleasant surroundings. To enjoy the riches of the earth and to do what I can to stop it being vandalised. I love art, but it's only in the last few years that I've taken an interest in paintings other than the pictures of ships which I've collected for some time. You grew up surrounded by masterpieces, I imagine?'—addressing Henry.

The other man nodded. 'Although I don't think either my brother or I paid much attention to them as boys. We regarded them rather like wallpaper.'

He began to describe some of the paintings at Bromsgrove Castle in which, now, he did take an interest.

A fraught moment came when, after picking at her main course, Atalanta put down her fork with most of the vegetable frittata she had chosen uneaten.

'Not good?' Oliver asked her, with an uplifted eyebrow.

'Yes, it's fine . . . I'm just not madly hungry.'

She opened the tortoiseshell box on a cord which was her evening bag and extracted a pack of cigarettes and a throw-away lighter.

'I wonder if you would mind not smoking here?' said Oliver. 'It can spoil other people's enjoyment of their food, so we try to keep it to the veranda and the terrace.'

It was a courteous request, but it made Atalanta explode.

'Oh, my God! So I'm a social pariah, polluting the air you saintly non-smokers have to breath!'

'Darling . . . darling . . .' Henry said soothingly, looking worried.

His wife drained her glass of wine and replaced it on the table with a thump. She pushed back her chair. 'I presume one is allowed to smoke in the loos here?' she said sarcastically, sweeping away from the table as, holding their napkins to them, the two men rose from their chairs.

'I'm sorry I've upset your wife,' said Oliver, as they sat down.

'Don't apologise, my dear chap. As a matter of fact I'm in favour of banning smoking in restaurants. Can't stand the habit. The fact is Atalanta's not herself at the moment. It's not long since she lost a baby—not for the first time, unfortunately—and that often leaves women jumpy and depressed for some time afterwards. Or so I'm told. That's why I brought her here . . . to cheer her up.'

Poor Atalanta! Laurian's always ready sympathy was instantly engaged by this revelation of the unhappiness behind the other woman's frivolous manner.

'I would go and see if she's all right, but I think that might make matters worse,' she said.

'Oh, she flares up but soon calms down. She'll be back when she's had a ciggy, as she calls it. She gave them up while she was pregnant, but after the miscarriage she started again. Have you ever smoked, Ann?'

'No, never. My father used to smoke cigars and I once tried

a few puffs——' She stopped short, for an anxious moment thinking she had given herself away.

Then she realised that a cigar-smoking father wasn't uncommon, and the time when she had tried it and made herself dizzy and sick had been long before Oliver's arrival.

The three of them finished their food and continued to chat; but for Laurian and, she felt sure, for the others as well, the evening had been spoiled by Atalanta's tantrum.

Suddenly she reappeared, smiling as if nothing had happened. 'Come and dance, Henry.'

For some time the earliest diners had been leaving their tables to dance before returning for puddings and coffee. The dance floor, a circle of polished stone surrounded by coral stone pillars wreathed with plumbago and coralita but open to the stars overhead, was within sight of the dining-room but not so close that the music made conversation an effort.

'Would you like to dance?' asked Oliver.

Laurian nodded, remembering how, earlier in the day, she had wondered what it would be like to be held by him. If the steel band continued to play their present slow rhythm, very soon she was going to find out.

However, before they arrived at the dance floor, the tempo changed to something faster and swingier. Couples who, moments ago, had been pressed close to each other, now drew apart and began to move separately.

Laurian had always loved dancing. As well as a modern record-player on which to listen to grand opera and symphonies, Archie had owned an old-fashioned wind-up gramphone with a cornucopia speaker and a collection of records going back to the Twenties. He had taught her to Charleston. By herself, she had played *The Dying Swan*, imagining herself to be Pavlova. The veranda had been the stage of theatres all over the world and she the great Russian ballerina, making audiences weep at the pathos of her performance.

Now, the airy folds of her new dress swaying with the fluid movements of her shoulders and hips, she danced to the catchy beat of the music of the islands.

Oliver didn't exert himself as much as some of the men on the floor. His style was relaxed, even indolent. Although she was not in his arms, he held her with his eyes. She found she couldn't look away from his almost hypnotic stare. Once or twice it left her face and moved downwards over her body, then back up again to re-engage her gaze. She saw very plainly that he found her desirable, but what he might do about it she had no idea.

The dance ended. In a brief pause, some people left the floor and others remained where they were; some of the older men discreetly patting their faces with expensive linen handkerchiefs, the women unable to do anything about moist upper lips and temples.

Laurian put up her hands to lift her thick hair away from the nape of her neck. She raised her face to the sky, now sparking with stars. The rum she had drunk before dinner, and the wine with it, the throbbing beat of the music, the balmy Caribbean night; all had gone to her head, making her feel alive in a way she never had in England.

As she stood cooling down, star-gazing, a hard arm circled her waist and Oliver drew her against him. But, as the music began, and she felt his thigh press against hers, ready to move in unison, Atalanta appeared with Henry behind her.

'May we change partners for this one? I want to apologise to Oliver for biting his head off!'

Over Henry Buckland's shoulder, Laurian watched his wife's long garnet-red nails moving lightly against the white cloth of

Oliver's dinner jacket.

From the top of some of the stone columns, spotlights partially concealed by foliage threw dappled shafts of radiance over the dancers. Atalanta's blonde hair caught the light, as did the diamonds surrounding the emerald of her engagement ring. She seemed to be gently massaging one of Oliver's vertebrae. At any moment Laurian expected to see those perfectly manicured fingers begin to play with the thick dark hair above the collar of his snowy voile dress shirt.

Laurian averted her eyes, dismayed to find herself wrung with jealousy. How could this be? Had Oliver's brief account of the tragic story of Judy so changed her feelings towards him that she was now on the verge of falling in love with him?

You were in love with him before, an innermost self reminded her. Nonsense: a child of thirteen can't be seriously in love. *Why not? Juliet was in love with Romeo.* Juliet wasn't a real person. *Shakespeare knew human nature, nobody better.* It was only calf love . . . an adolescent phase. *Perhaps, but that was then . . . this is now. Who else have you ever met to compare with Oliver? Don't say Robert.*

Robert. For the first time since breakfast, which seemed a long time ago, more like ten days than ten hours, Laurian remembered Robert and his nightly telephone call to report on his father's condition and ask how she had spent her day. What would he have thought when the switchboard operator at Emerald Beach told him that not only was Miss Ford not in her room, she wasn't in the hotel. She was out, and they couldn't say what time she might come back.

'I'm afraid I'm not much of a dancer,' Henry said apologetically.

'Would you rather sit out? You must be quite tired after snorkeling nearly all day. Did you bring your own mask or borrow one from the hotel?' Laurian asked, feeling it was about time she showed some interest in him instead of going off in a trance of private thought.

'I brought my own.' He steered her to the edge of the floor where they left the slow-moving cluster of embraced couples and went back to their table.

It was some time before the others returned. Henry and Laurian were eating delicious home-made coconut ice cream embedded with nuts and slivers of crystallised fruit, when they saw Atalanta coming back.

With her full unsupported breasts outlined by the backless black top, and the clinging folds of a white silk jersey skirt showing the lines of her hips and thighs, she drew many glances. Watching her, Laurian felt sure Oliver must have found the close pressure of Atalanta's body a far more inflaming experience than his brief contact with her own slighter figure.

At one time she had thought she was never going to have any bosom and was doomed to remain as flat-chested as when *Neptune's Daughter* was painted. Eventually she had grown breasts and her first bras, worn in hope rather than expectation, had stopped shooting up to her neck when she raised her arms. But even though she was satisfied with her bosom, it didn't compare with Atalanta's. Perhaps she had only imagined the look in Oliver's eyes when they were dancing.

Watching him draw out Atalanta's chair, Laurian wondered what he had done with *Neptune's Daughter*. She had almost forgotten its existence. Had he got rid of it? Or was it still somewhere in the house? She wondered what use he had made of Archie's library, her favourite room. Probably it was now one of the public parts of the hotel. She hoped there would be an opportunity, later, to go and look.

Since taking full possession of the upper floors of the house in Spitalfields, she had often thought how well some of the leather-bound books from Kingscote Abbey would look in her panelled sitting-room.

Had she been in Oliver's place, she would have filled a box with books and had it shipped to the child she had dispossessed. Obviously, it hadn't occurred to him that a girl, half mermaid, half bookworm, would miss her favourite books almost as much as she missed the warm sea by day and the sound of the cicadas at night.

'Not for me. I'll have coffee . . . black,' said Atalanta, when her husband advised her to try the ice cream. She looked across the table at Laurian. 'I suppose, being what Henry's old Nanny calls "one of Pharaoh's lean kine", you can eat anything you please. I have to be frightfully self-disciplined.'

'I ought to be,' said her husband, patting his middle which carried more flesh than it should for a man of his age. 'You look in good trim, Thornham. How do you manage it?'

'I take a good deal of exercise and normally I dine in my quarters, rather more sparingly than I have this evening,' said Oliver. 'Would you care to dance again, Ann?' By now she had finished her ice.

What prompted her to refuse, she wasn't sure. Part of her wanted to dance with him. Part of her counselled: Don't. Stay out of his arms.

She said, 'To be honest, I don't find the sandals which Atalanta very kindly lent me all that comfortable for dancing. As I told you this afternoon, I don't often wear high heels and these heels are extra high. I'd hate to twist my ankle . . . or possibly snap a strap on your Maud Frizons, Atalanta,' she added, the insoles of the sandals being stamped with the name of a very expensive Bond Street shoe shop.

Oliver accepted her excuse without comment, but the look in his eyes suggested he didn't believe it.

'Shall we have our coffee on the terrace?' suggested Henry. 'Then my wife can have a cigarette. I shouldn't really encourage you in the habit,' he said to her, 'but I know you won't enjoy your coffee without one.'

Laurian was forming the impression that theirs was the kind of marriage in which Henry had to curry favour with Atalanta to keep their relationship sweet. She thought he was making a mistake. Atalanta might well prefer it if he laid down the law and told her he couldn't stand living with a smoker and she would have to cut it out.

On the terrace many of the comfortable white cane sofas and armchairs were already occupied. But in a group seating six round a low glass table, four places were still free and the couple already there had evidently met and talked to the Bucklands before.

The husband stood up when he saw them. 'Come and join us,' the wife invited.

Introductions were made; coffee and liqueurs ordered. Laurian found herself sitting next to Mona—she hadn't caught their surname—who was Canadian.

After giving Laurian a résumé of their history—she and Steve were from Vancouver and, tired of the apartment on Maui, one of the Hawaiian islands, which had been their vacation place for the past five years, had decided to try someplace else—Mona asked, 'Have you and Oliver been here before?' It was clear she took them for a pair.

It was a natural mistake in a set-up where not many women of Laurian's age were likely to be there alone.

Laurian was seated on one of the sofas with Oliver beside her, the Bucklands on the sofa opposite, and the two Canadians now in the chairs at right angles to them, like the host and hostess at a table. Oliver was sitting with one arm stretched along the top of the back cushions, behind Laurian's shoulders, a posture which might have supported Mona's impression that they were partners.

He leaned forward and closer to Laurian to say to the Canadian woman, 'I live here, but it's Ann's first time here.' He looked into Laurian's eyes. 'That is right, isn't it? You haven't been here before?'

Did he know who she was? Had he recognised her?

CHAPTER FOUR

AS OLIVER waited for her answer, Laurian wished she had never begun her masquerade. But even if he knew, this was hardly the moment to admit she wasn't Ann Ford. If he didn't, it would be a shock and not something to be discussed in front of Mona and the others. It seemed better, if not to lie, at least to prevaricate.

'I—I have been in the Caribbean before . . . not at the Emerald Beach,' she answered. 'The hotel where I'm staying is along the coast on the big island,' she explained to the Canadian woman.

'I see. Do you like it there?' asked Mona.

'Yes, it's fine . . . very comfortable. Not up to the standard here, but a very pleasant place to stay.'

'And where else in the Caribbean have you been, Ann?'

'I've stayed in Antigua,' Laurian told her, not untruthfully. 'Are the Hawaiian islands very different from these islands?'

To her relief this question prompted a detailed description of Maui and the apartment Steve and Mona had owned there.

Although he gave no sign of restlessness, Laurian sensed that inwardly Oliver was bored by this. For her own part, although in the normal way she was always interested in hearing about faraway places, tonight she was not in the mood to listen to travellers' tales.

When she had finished her coffee and it was possible to get a word in edgeways, she said, 'I think I ought to be getting back to my hotel.'

'Yes, perhaps you should,' said Oliver, with alacrity. 'Would you excuse us, Mona?'

As the two of them rose from the sofa, the others broke off their separate conversation and Laurian thanked the Bucklands for dinner. She debated inviting them to join her for dinner one evening, but decided they would prefer to stay where they were.

'If I don't see you again, I hope you enjoy the rest of your holiday . . . and you too, Steve.'

'Thank you, Ann. I'm sorry there hasn't been time for us to get to know each other,' the Canadian said, with the friendliness which seemed characteristic of most North Americans.

'I'll give your sandals to Oliver when I've changed back into my espadrilles. Thanks very much for lending them to me,' were Laurian's last words to Atalanta.

'Not at all. It was fun running into you.'

Accompanying Laurian into the house, Olive said, 'While you're changing your shoes, I'll get out of this gear. I shan't be five minutes.'

'Are you taking me back?' She had thought he meant to walk her to the jetty but that she would be taken back by a guard or some other employee.

'It's the least I can do, don't you think?'

Not quite sure what he meant, she watched him spring up the staircase, taking the shallow steps three at a time.

In the shower room adjoining the shop, where she had left her other clothes, Laurian took off her dress and folded it carefully to fit the carrier Mary Poole had given her for it. Once more in her shirt and shorts, with the beige espadrilles on her feet, she left the boutique and returned to the hall where Oliver was coming downstairs in a pair of the pale khaki trousers Americans called chinos and a dark red cotton-knit sports shirt with the Lacoste alligator on the chest.

Seeing the bronze kid sandals dangling from her hand, he said, 'Bring those along to the desk and Theo, our night porter, will give them to the maid on duty.'

Taking the carrier from her, he led the way down the corridor which passed the library. Like all the principal rooms, it had tall heavy double doors which, in her time, had always stood open. Now they were closed.

Noticing her glance towards them, Oliver said, 'That was, and still is, Archibald Bradford's library.'

He didn't offer to show it to her, making her wonder uneasily if he *had* guessed who she was, or if, by asking if she had been here before, he had meant the West Indies in general.

The reception area at the far end of the corridor was another addition to the building. The man on duty at the desk was in his fifties, but she didn't remember ever seeing him before. Not that she and Archie had ever spent much time on the big island, apart from periodic visits to St James, the one sizeable town, for supplies.

'I'm taking one of the boats to run my guest back to Emerald Beach, Theo. I'm not sure how long I'll be gone.'

'Very good, sir. Goodnight, ma'am.'

As they left the fan-cooled interior and returned to the warm night outside, Laurian wondered if Oliver's reference to her as 'my guest' rather than 'Miss Ford' was because he knew she wasn't Miss Ford.

Perhaps she was being too quick to read nervous-making implications into everything he said; such as *why* he wasn't sure how long he would be gone. He must have done the run to Emerald Beach many times and know to a minute how long it took, there and back. Was he planning to stop on the way? There wasn't anywhere to stop.

The coast of the larger island between here and her hotel was heavily overgrown with lush vegetation. There were one or two mangrove-lined inlets which she had explored as a child, imagining herself on an expedition to the great swamps of South America. But the mangrove coves would be eerie places at night—they were fairly creepy by day with their strange aerial roots growing downwards into the water—and no doubt infested by mosquitoes.

'How did you manage to get rid of mosquitoes here?' she asked, remembering Atalanta's remark and realising that she had no itchy places on her ankles. Under tables was a favourite place for the female mosquitoes to lurk. 'There always used to be plenty of them,' was on the tip of her tongue, but she managed to substitute, 'I thought they were part and parcel of the tropics.'

'They are, but not where there's no stagnant water for breeding; and we're far enough away from the big island to prevent them commuting, I'm glad to say.'

The jetty was in the small place—out of sight of the house—but in the intervening years it had been transformed into a small marina with various sailing and power boats moored along pontoon walkways illumined by powerful arc lights.

The night porter must have telephoned a watchman. Wearing a white boiler suit with the *PR* logo, he was waiting for them by a small launch with, Laurian noticed, what amounted to a comfortably cushioned sofa in the stern.

Oliver stepped inboard first and turned to give her a hand. The firm clasp of his fingers reminded her of his arm tightening round her on the dance floor and how, for a moment, before Atalanta's advent, she had felt herself caught and held fast by the superior strength of a tall and muscular man. Not an unpleasant sensation, however much feminists more aggressive than herself might deplore female subservience in any circumstances.

The watchman, who was almost as tall as Oliver but built like a barrel, unfastened the mooring line and tossed it aboard.

'Thanks, Tiny. See you later.'

As Oliver started the motor, from old habit Laurian picked up the line and coiled it, using her elbow.

Glancing over his shoulder, he saw what she was doing. 'You're used to "messing about in boats", I gather?'

'I've done a bit of sailing.'

Had his allusion to *The Wind In The Willows* been coincidental, or did he remember that, finding their library lacked a copy of Kenneth Grahame's masterpiece, he had made her a present of a copy he had on *Euphrosyne?* He had got it back when she left. She had left it behind—with the page he had incribed *To Laurie from Ol* torn out. It was the only time in her life she had ever damaged a book.

Ol. What a horrible diminutive of his knightly name! It surprised her now that he had allowed her to call him that.

Turning the boat in the direction which would take them past the house, he raised his voice to say, 'Boats aren't allowed past the main beach during the day, but it's all right at night and the house looks a fine sight lit up.'

It did indeed. She had never seen anything more romantic than the handsome stone mansion with most of its windows alight and the terrace bathed in the glow of candles and Japanese lanterns.

'It looks more like a private house, where a ball is in progress, than a hotel,' she told him.

'That's rather the object of the exercise.' He cut their speed so that, above the quietened hum of the engine, they could hear the music drifting across the water.

The band was repeating the theme from *Out of Africa*, reminding Laurian of the ecstasy and tragedy of that long-ago love affair, and the tears she had shed in the darkness of the cinema. Now the evocative music, the moonlit island, her sad-happy memories of her father, all caught at her heart and brought fresh tears to her eyes. Deep emotions, for years subliminated by her attention to her career, had this evening been brought to the surface; especially the tender longings of an adolescent girl falling in love for the first time.

'Someone's waving. Looks like our garrulous visitor from Vancover.' Oliver lifted a hand in response to the fluttering motion from the terrace.

Gently he increased throttle and the boat surged ahead more strongly, spreading a train of foam across the placid surface of the lagoon. Soon the house was no more than a glimpse of golden lights flickering between the trunks of a grove of palms.

As they turned in a sweeping curve round the end of the island, he took something from his pocket and tossed it to her in the stern. It was a small plastic bottle.

'Anti-mozz lotion. Better rub some on your arms and legs.'

In preparation for an interlude among the mangroves? she wondered, her heart beginning to thump with much the same nervous excitement she had felt on the way home after her first date with Neal Lingfield's best friend.

Young men, other than her two foster-brothers, had been unknown quantities then. Oliver Thornham still was. She had a feeling that nothing she had learnt since her first kiss would help her to cope with Oliver's kisses—if that was what he had in mind.

It seemed that it wasn't. Veering from a straight line only when it was necessary to avoid submerged rocks, he kept the boat skimming directly towards the headland and, from there, towards the lights of her hotel.

However, to her surprise, instead of making for the Emerald Beach jetty, he steered for the centre of the beach, expertly shutting off the engine at a point which kept the boat going by its own momentum until it was in shallow water.

There, regardless of his trousers, he swung himself over the side and hauled the boat further in until she was lightly beached at the bows.

'No need for you to get wet.'

Before Laurian could follow suit, he plucked her out of the well and carried her ashore.

It was years since, fooling around at a party with a gang of fellow art students, she had been swept off her feet by a boisterious character called Rolf. That had been a game. This wasn't; at least not for her. She was trembling when he set her down.

'You haven't got your dress.' He turned away to retrieve the forgotten carrier. 'There you are.'

'Thank you . . . and thank you for bringing me back. Goodnight, Oliver.'

He didn't reply but stood looking down at her in silence. Laurian found she couldn't move and could scarcely breathe.

Then he put his hands on either side of her waist and bent his tall head and touched his lips to her mouth.

It was the most delicate of kisses; so light that, had she been asleep, it wouldn't have woken her. Then he kissed her again and still it was gentle, but the soft movements of his lips sent a shudder of exquisite feeling through every nerve in her body. If he kissed her a third time . . .

But he didn't. His hands left her waist and he straightened and stepped away.

'Goodnight . . . Ann.'

Seconds later, he was up to his ankles in the sea. Half a minute later he was shoving the boat off the sand. A minute later he was waving goodbye and heading back the way he had come.

And although he hadn't said goodbye, and his kisses had been a beginning, not an ending, there had been no mention of when they would meet again.

'*Who* was that *gorgeous* hunk of beefcake who brought you back?' enquired Mrs Porter Lansing who, with a number of other people, had witnessed Laurian's return.

Laurian would have preferred it if Oliver's way of saying goodnight had been unobserved. It was bound to cause comment and probably a good deal of banter. But she found that she minded more his being described as beefcake, a term which, in her vocabulary, meant much brawn and little brain. He was big. He was strong. But no one was less like the over-muscled, pin-witted stud the term beefcake conjured in her mind.

However, she managed to smile as she answered, 'He's English. Did you enjoy your trip to St James?'

'There's not too much there . . . just a market and a few shops, but the people were all very friendly and I bought some gifts for my daughter and her children,' said Connie Lansing.

'What'll you have to drink, Ann?' Melvin Dorado came up behind her and put his hand on her shoulder.

'Nothing for me at the moment, thanks, Mel. I'm going to bed. Have you two met?'

'We sure have . . . I was sitting right there,'— pointing to the chair next to Connie's—'before I went to the john.'

'And missed seeing the real handsome guy who brought Ann back from wherever she's been today . . . and kissed her right there on the beach,' Connie informed him, pointing to the spot where it had happened. 'Where did you go today, honey?'

'To one of the other hotels.' Laurian didn't intend to reveal which one. 'I'm glad you found some nice presents. I must go to St James myself some time. See you both at breakfast. Goodnight.'

As she walked away, she heard Connie say to Mel, 'I don't think we'll see much of her from now on. It's nice she's found herself a guy. At her age, a vacation's no fun by yourself . . . at any age, I guess . . .'

In the lobby the manager, Edgar Headley, was behind the reception desk, standing in the doorway of the office where the switchboard girls worked their shifts.

When he saw Laurian heading for the staircase leading to her room on the upper floor of the long low building, he stopped her by saying, 'Oh, Miss Ford . . . there was a call for you earlier. Mr Adstock telephoned from England. He said he'd call back in the morning.'

'Thank you, Mr Headley. Goodnight.'

Later, sitting up in bed, trying to read one of the books she had bought after first seeing Oliver and not recognising the mature, clean-shaven man about town as the bearded yachtsman in his twenties she had known beforetime—the local word for a time that was past and gone came into her head as naturally as if she had never lost her familiarity with the big island's dialect—she found it impossible to concentrate.

Closing the book, she put it aside on the night table and switched off the reading lamp. Before she lay down, she peeled off her nightdress and tossed it to the foot of the divan. The sheet was more than enough covering when the air-conditioning, which she didn't like, was turned off and the door to the balcony opened. Mosquitoes were a problem here, but when she had told the receptionist she preferred to sleep with her windows open, she had been supplied with a small gadget which plugged into a power point and heated a pastille which effectively kept the bloodthirsty female mosquitoes from entering the room.

Judging by the absence of drone from other air-conditioning units, no one else in the hotel had gone to bed yet. Laurian could hear the rustling of the palm tree outside her room and the distant sound of the sea breaking on the reef.

Lying with closed eyes, she could almost feel Oliver's kisses, especially the second one. It made her quiver inside to remember it. What would have happened if they had been somewhere secluded and she had put her arms round his neck and clung to him, as she had wanted to? On the strength of those two gentle kisses, she had wanted him to make love to her; wanted it desperately.

So I must *not* see him again, she told herself. I'm altogether too vulnerable. I can't rely on myself to keep him at arm's length.

Why must you? the reasonable voice of her *alter ego* enquired.

Because I'm already involved with Robert . . . and short-lived affairs aren't my style. *You aren't committed to Robert: not yet . . . and why should an affair with Oliver be short-lived? It might last a lifetime.*

How could it? His life is here. Mine is in London. Even if I were prepared to give up my career for him—and it wouldn't be a minor sacrifice—I couldn't just drop *Laurian*. I have people depending on me; not only the ones who work for me but their families as well. If I opted out, they would all be in trouble. I couldn't do that to them.

Knowing that if she had any sense at all she wouldn't see Oliver again, she forced herself to stop thinking about him and tried a trick which was supposed to be a quick soporific; counting backwards from a thousand.

'Where were you when I rang up last night?' Robert sounded aggrieved.

'I ran into a customer and she and her husband asked me to have dinner with them at their hotel. I'm sorry you wasted a call. How's your father?'

'Not too good.'

'Oh, dear, I thought he was improving.'

'He was,' explained Robert, 'but yesterday his condition took a down-turn. I don't know whether he's going to make it or not. I don't think anyone does. What else did you do yesterday besides dining with these people?'

'I went for a sail.'

'Who with?'

'No one. By myself.'

'I didn't know you knew how to handle a boat. Where did you learn that?'

'I used to sail at school,' she told him.

This was true. In the grounds of her boarding school, originally a large country house, there had been a lake, and sailing had been part of the curriculum. Not that Laurian had needed tuition in a skill she had learned from Archie at such a young age that it seemed to be something she had always known how to do, like breathing.

'I hope you wore a life-jacket,' said Robert.

'I was sailing inside the reef and there wasn't a chance of capsizing. There was barely enough wind. What's the weather like there?'

'Bloody awful,' he said morosely. 'God, what I'd give to be out there in the sun with you!'

'Poor you . . . it is a shame,' she said sympathetically. 'How's your mother bearing up?'

They talked for several more minutes, Robert bemoaning his predicament, Laurian commiserating.

After he had rung off, she realised that although she was genuinely sorry for him, trapped by filial duty in a place he loathed with parents with whom he had little in common, it was no use pretending she missed him. Connie Lansing's statement that a holiday on one's own was no fun at any age wasn't entirely true, she thought.

If it turned out that Robert was unable to join her, she would be content to spend her days windsurfing and her evenings chatting to people like Connie and Mel. Indeed, from a purely selfish point of view, she hoped he would decide to postpone his holiday until later in the winter. Even if he hadn't been bowed down with family worries at the moment, it would be impossible to explain, in a transatlantic telephone call, that she knew now, with certainty, they could never be more than friends. But she would have to make that plain to him as soon as she saw him again. Even though the feelings Oliver had aroused in her last night could never be fulfilled, they made any other relationship unthinkable.

After breakfast, before going to borrow a surfboard, she went back to her room to write to the Bucklands, thanking them for their hospitality. She was addressing the envelope when her telephone rang again.

There could be only one reason why Robert would ring back so soon. His father must have died.

But it wasn't Robert's voice which answered her heart-sinking, 'Hello?'

'Good morning. Oliver here. I'm taking a couple of people—not the Bucklands—sailing today. Would you care to join us? We'll be starting out about eleven, lunching on board, and coming back about five.'

Not giving herself time to think about it, Laurian said, 'It's nice of you to suggest it, but I've already made arrangements for today.'

'You couldn't rearrange them?'

'I'm afraid not.'

'Too bad. I think you'd like the Sheridans. They're two young American lawyers who've been coming here for several years. This time is, in fact, their honeymoon, but as they've been sharing an apartment for four years, they're happy to mix with other people some of the time. How about joining us for dinner tonight?'

'I'm afraid I can't manage that either. I—I'm going into St James with some people I've made friends with here.'

'I see.'

There was silence at the other end of the line. Laurian hoped he wouldn't ask where she was dining in St James. One white lie was enough; she didn't want to be forced to embroider it.

'I hope you enjoy your sail,' she said, thinking how much she would have enjoyed it herself, but thankful she had refused the invitation at once, before her resolution weakened.

'I expect we shall . . . although a foursome would have been more fun,' said Oliver. 'Have a good time at whatever it is you're doing today.' Something in his tone made her wonder if he suspected her of inventing a prior engagement.

'Thanks . . . goodbye.' As she said it, she had a depressing feeling it probably was the last time she would ever speak to him.

She hoped he might say *'Au revoir'* or *'Ciao'*. No, he wouldn't say *'Ciao'* except if he were in Italy. Anywhere else it had the ring of affectation. Robert had picked up the habit from cronies in advertising and to hear him use it always set her teeth on edge . . . one of the small irritations which, taken together, had made her hold back from the closer partnership he wanted.

'Goodbye.'

There was a click and the line went dead. Slowly Laurian replaced the receiver on its rest.

She had done the right thing, the sensible thing. But it didn't make her feel good.

'Watching you skim around on that board is like watching ballet on TV,' said Connie. 'You're so slim and graceful. Is that the new swimsuit you bought in St James yesterday?'

Laurian gave an affirmative, 'Uh-huh' and then added, 'Thank you' for the compliment.

'What I'd give for a figure like yours—not that it'd do me much good unless I had a new face to go with it,' said Connie, yelling with laughter at her own joke and waking Mel, stretched out beside her, out of his afternoon nap.

Laurian's new one-piece was the colour of a Cos lettuce, setting off a tan which every day deepened a tone. She would never return to the deep coffee-brown she had been as a child; one had to live in the sun to become that colour, and she hoped she hadn't damaged her skin by all that early sun bathing. Now she was taking care to protect her face from the most damaging rays, although not, like some of the women at the hotel, by using a total sun-block *and* a shady hat.

'You're a sight for sore eyes, Ann,' said Mel, rubbing a hand over his. 'Did you enjoy yourself out there? I wouldn't mind having a try at it, but I doubt I could get that darned sail up out of the water.'

'Ann'll give you a lesson if you ask nicely,' said Connie. 'Seeing you fall off the board would make a change from watching that girl make a clown of herself.'

Laurian glanced along the beach. In the shade of a manchineel tree, a girl in her early twenties was having her hair finely plaited and beaded in an Afro style by one of the local beach traders.

Although there were no private beaches on the island, the hotel discouraged traders from pestering the guests. Most of them didn't. Two women from a nearby village strolled along every morning with armfuls of sun-dresses, beach wraps and beads. A man with souvenirs came by at about the same time, and another man with a case of cheap jewellery and watches appeared most days but didn't attempt to hard-sell if visitors showed no interest in his wares.

However, there were also several young men who were more persistent and who, as well as pressing the sale of trinkets, would try to sweet-talk any woman, regardless of age, if she looked susceptible.

Laurian had heard the maids discussing this. When they chatted among themselves, most visitors couldn't understand all they said, but she could—and could speak the same dialect, did they but know it. She had found out during her schooldays that she had a quick ear for accents and tricks of speech. It had been her ability to take off the teaching staff's voices which had first won her friends after an initial period when a combination of shyness and grief had made her seem offputtingly reserved.

'That no-good spree-boy, Fletcher, he chat down anyone, man, don' matter how old she be,' she had heard one of the older maids say disapprovingly. Laurian had passed by, wondering why it was chatting up in England and chatting down here. In her view, as much blame attached to women who encouraged such advances as to the young men concerned.

The girl who was having her hair done in public was not the subject of censure among the other women guests because she made eyes at the local lads. She wasn't liked for several reasons, the chief one being that she looked so pleased with herself as she undulated from beach to bar and back again in her highest of high-cut swimsuits and her gold ankle-chain.

Before Laurian went to the poolside bar to quench the thirst she had worked up windsurfing, she dabbled her feet in the salt-water footbath and wrapped herself in another of yesterday's purchases, a length of thin cotton patterned with swirls of saffron and apricot on white.

Had it not been for thoughts of what she might have been doing instead, she would have enjoyed her visit to the island's greatly expanded main town. But last night she had hardly slept for thinking of Oliver, and all today thoughts of him had kept slipping into her mind, try as she would to keep them out.

Tactfully, Connie and Mel had not remarked on the fact that, after kissing her good night the day before yesterday, her 'gorgeous hunk' hadn't been seen again.

At the bar were the usual group whose daily routine consisted of making their first appearance about mid-morning, visibly hungover; lying on sun-beds till lunchtime when the first rum punch of the day began to revive them and thereafter propping up the bar until it was time to dress up for the nightly rave-up, each night at a different hotel.

The only time any of them used the pool was for a quick cool off, each immersion adding to the film of sun oil around the pool's edge which a garden boy in a knitted beret would be cleaning off the pale blue tiles when Laurian passed by for her pre-breakfast dip in the sea.

The king of the court at the bar was the partner of the girl with the anklet. Almost never without a glass in his hand, and with an apparently inexhaustible fund of tall tales and funny stories, he kept the others in fits of uproarious laughter but didn't amuse the people who wanted to relax by the pool without having to listen to a chorus of guffaws.

Laurian asked the barman for a tall glass of iced water with the juice of a fresh lime. Every meal at the hotel began with the pink-frocked waitresses going round the dining-room with jugs of cold water and she always drank at least two glasses, knowing the island's tap water to be as drinkable as any in England, although some guests eyed it dubiously.

Rather than perching on a bar stool, probably being bidden to join the group, several of whom had given her interested glances when their own women weren't looking, she took her drink to a quiet corner of the garden and sat in the circle of shade cast by a sunbrella covered with long green strands of plastic 'grass'.

Oliver would never permit such an eyesore in his grounds, she thought, remembering the elegance of the garden furniture at the Palm Reef Club. Of course it might be that he had commissioned a top-flight decorator to help him, but even so the best decorators didn't impose their own taste; they were interpreters of their clients' tastes, although their signature was nearly always recognisable to a trained eye.

Dammit! I'm thinking about him *again*, she realised, angry with herself for lacking the mental discipline to exclude him from her mind.

The heart has its reasons, which are quite unknown to the head.

Probably the quotation came to her at that moment because, on the way past the pool, she had noticed a woman reading one of the many books about the Duke and Duchess of Windsor which had been published following the Duchess's death.

In the days when Laurian had spent a lot of time in second-hand bookshops, adding to her collection of books about the great fashion designers, *The Heart Has Its Reasons*, the Duchess of Windsor's own account of their love story, had been a title which had often caught her eye on the shelves.

Whether they had been right or wrong to marry would always be a matter of debate, like the truth about Mary Queen of Scots' ill-fated marriage to the Earl of Bothwell.

The problem of whether to follow one's heart or one's head was something which every woman, faced with a conflict between the two, had to decide for herself. Other people's choice weren't any help; if anything they only confused the issue.

Laurian sipped the refreshingly sharp-tasting lime drink, the ice cubes floating at the brim brushing her upper lip, reminding her of the equally light but warm touch of Oliver's first goodnight kiss.

Frazma. The island term for mental turmoil popped up from the depths of her memory, a word she hadn't heard for years but which summed up perfectly the state she was in at present.

One of the hotel receptionists, who had been following the path to the swimming pool, saw Laurian sitting under the sunbrella and changed direction.

'A letter for you, Miss Ford. The boy who brought it said it was urgent.'

'Thank you.'

The envelope had the Palm Reef logo on the flap. Could it be a note from Atalanta? She should have received Laurian's thank-you letter this morning, but why should she want to meet again when the Club offered plenty of interesting holiday acquaintances?

The note wasn't from Atalanta. It was from Oliver. The sight of his signature, written in black ink with a nib which emphasised the decisive character of his handwriting, made her fingers tremble and caused the sheet of expensively crisp ivory laid paper to quiver like a leaf in the wind.

'May I borrow the iron and ironing board, please?' Laurian asked the same receptionist who had delivered Oliver's note to her.

'Certainly, Miss Ford. A maid will do some pressing for you, if you prefer?'

'I'm quite happy to do it myself, thanks.'

'I'll have someone take it to your room right away.'

On reaching her bedroom, Laurian left the door ajar and went out on to the balcony, which was furnished with two cane chairs and a glass-topped cane table.

For the sixth or seventh time in the past forty minutes, she re-read Oliver's letter.

> *Dear Ann,*
>
> *Once a week I give a drinks party in the library to introduce guests whom I think will have things in common but who might not meet each other during their time here. We are expecting Richard Lucas whom I think you might like to talk to.*
>
> *If you would like to come over this evening, a boat will be sent to pick you up at 6.45 p.m. I am off island today, so would you please speak to John Lynn.*
>
> *I hope to see you later.*
>
> *Oliver.*

Much as she longed to see what the library was like now, Laurian could—just!—have resisted that lure. But a chance to meet Richard Lucas, the American designer whom she admired above all others, was impossible to pass up.

She had already rung John Lynn to accept the invitation from the telephone at the desk. Now, waiting for the ironing board to arrive, she wondered if there were some way she could reveal who she was to Richard Lucas without letting Oliver know . . . if he didn't already. She still wasn't sure about that. Nor was she sure why he had asked her to the party.

It could be an act of altruistic kindness because he realised that an introduction to Lucas must thrill any unknown designer, which was what he took her to be. Or it could be that he wanted to see her again.

A tap on the bedroom door heralded the entrance of one of the maids.

You pressing' a special dress for the jump up tonight, ma'am?' she asked, as she set up the board.

The Emerald Beach was having its weekly barbecue followed by dancing to music by a local group.

Laurian explained that she had been invited out.

'Oh, that's too bad,' said the maid. 'You is goin' to miss a real good time. Two of the boys in the band is family to me and they is the best group on this island.'

In the light of Robert's instructions, Laurian had brought only one summer evening outfit with her. It was six years old: made for her twentieth birthday, the last birthday she had celebrated with her adopted family in Yorkshire.

The top was a piece of exquisite Edwardian black lace she had found in a junk shop and made up into a collarless shirt of the utmost simplicity. The skirt was from the same source, a late Victorian petticoat of fine white cambric to which she had attached extra ruffles of broderie anglaise and yards of white insertion through which she had threaded narrow black silk ribbons, tied in bows at the front. The whole thing had cost a song, yet she never wore it without receiving compliments and enquiries as to whether it was from her current collection.

By half past six she was ready; her hair washed, her eyes made up, a pair of tiny ivory hearts, given to her by David, her eldest foster-brother, swinging on fine gold chains from the lobes of her ears.

As her flesh-coloured bras no longer matched the amber-gold of her skin, and even the flimsiest bra could be seen through the delicate meshes, she was naked under the black shirt, although the design of the lace did not make this immediately apparent. Leaving the top two buttons, which were small beads of jet, unfastened, she was wearing a spiky collar of shells and coral bought in St James the day before.

The boat from Palm Reef was waiting at the hotel jetty when she arrived there a few minutes early. It was the guard called Josh who had been deputed to fetch her. This time he smiled when he saw her.

'Good evenin', miss.'

Laurian smiled back at him. 'Good evening.'

She had a feeling that, about eighteen years ago, Josh had been one of the boys who had sometimes swum out to the small island and been entertained by Archie and herself. She wondered if he remembered the little girl who had lived there then. Probably not.

'How long have you worked for Mr Thornham?' she asked him, on the way over.

'Nine years, miss.'

Receiving polite replies to all her questions but unable to get a conversation going, Laurian gave up the attempt and thought about the American designer she was shortly going to meet.

It had been said of Richard Lucas that he was the downtown guy who had made it possible for every woman to look like an uptown girl.

In New York he had recently transformed a store furnished with English and American antiques into an appropriate background for the Richard Lucas look.

In London, his shop in Bond Street had the atmosphere of a country house library, and girls who bought their clothes there, even if they lived in a semi-detached in the suburbs, looked as if, on Friday afternoon, they would be leaving the city to return to their natural habitat, a large country house surrounded by Daddy's ancestral acres.

Laurian's aims as a designer were somewhat different from Richard Lucas's, but he was one of the people she admired most in her field.

To her surprise, Oliver was waiting on the dock when the boat slid alongside. He and Josh helped her to step ashore and, after she had thanked the West Indian for bringing her, Oliver, who had kept hold of her hand, surprised her again by kissing it, in the French manner, and saying, 'You don't need me to tell you you look stunning, but I will. Is that something you designed yourself?'

'Thank you . . . yes, it is.' She would have freed her fingers, but he wouldn't allow it, keeping her hand firmly enclosed in his.

'I think you must be more successful than I realised,' he said. 'Even I, knowing little about women's clothes, can see that your dress is a knock-out.'

'Thank you again.'

'As you must have noticed, the night you dined here, most women, having worked on a tan, seem to feel compelled to display as much of it as possible in the evening,' said Oliver. 'I don't mind bare flesh on the beach. If, on European beaches, women want to strip to the waist like men, I don't object to that either. But I sometimes wish more of them realised, as you obviously do, that the female body is far more alluring when it's attractively wrapped—particularly in black lace.'

'Thank you,' she said, for the third time, wondering if he meant to hold hands all the way to the house.

It seemed that he did and, short of tugging hers free, there was nothing she could do about it. Did she want to? She knew she didn't.

'Is your VIP here now?' she asked.

'Yes . . . but keeping himself to himself in one of the cottages. Only the staff know he's here.'

'How long is Richard Lucas staying?'

'He's booked for five nights.'

Unable to think of anything else to say, Laurian fell silent, intensely aware of his hard palm and the latent power in the long fingers folded round hers.

The porter on duty in the lobby wasn't the one called Theo. He smiled and bowed as they passed. 'Good evenin', ma'am.'

She had expected to find the doors of the library standing open or, if not, being opened and closed by one of the staff as Oliver's guests presented themselves. She had formed the impression, from his note, that only a small selection of all those staying at the Club would be at the party.

However, the doors were closed and there was no one on duty outside them. Grasping one of the chased brass knobs Archie had found in a Paris flea market, Oliver paused to say, 'Most people who've seen it consider this room very fine. I got an English decorator to advise me on the redecoration, and I think he's done a splendid job.'

He opened the door, at the same time releasing her hand, and stood back for her to go in. Her heart in her mouth in case the room she had loved was barely recognisable, Laurian stepped across the threshold.

When, in a single swift glance, she took in what had been done to the place where some of her happiest hours had been spent, she came close to bursting into tears.

'Well . . . what do you think of it? asked Oliver, after some moments had passed since he had followed her into the library and closed the door.

She couldn't turn to look at him or he would see how much moved she was. Mastering her voice, she said quietly, 'I think it's the loveliest room I've ever seen.'

To her, it had always been that; even when it had been shabby and dusty, nothing in it repaired or renewed in the quarter of a century since her father had built the house.

She ought to have known that it would be all right; not spoilt, not tarted up in a way she couldn't have borne. There was a great deal more furniture than there had been before, but all of it perfectly in keeping with Archie's oiginal pieces.

The one thing the library had lacked, although she hadn't been conscious of it as a child but would have been now, was flowers. This flaw in its perfection had been remedied. Everywhere she looked there were flowers and even several small trees growing in pots inside giant wicker baskets. Some of the flowers were fresh and some were dried like the great armful of golden alchemilla filling the wide stone hearth which, in their day, had been piled high with cobwebby driftwood. Not that a fireplace had been necessary, but Archie had had one built because he liked the look of it.

Above the hearth had hung a huge giltwood mirror, the glass in it misty with age. This was no longer there. In its place, now handsomely framed, hung the portrait of her—*Neptune's Daughter*.

'And the portrait . . . do you like that?' Oliver asked, moving to stand alongside her. Before she could answer, he added, 'I've had more than one offer for it from connoisseurs who wanted to add it to their collections. It's by a Dutchman called Helder who, since he painted that, has become rather famous.'

Laurian considered saying, 'Really?' and turning her gaze

elsewhere. But the portrait, not seen for so long, exerted a kind of fascination, and something impelled her to say, 'And the little girl . . . who was she?'

'She used to live here,' he told her. 'Her name was Laurian Bradford . . . sometimes shortened to Ann Ford.'

A wave of colour swept up from her throat to her forehead. 'Atalanta told you.'

Oliver shook his head. 'I've known for certain who you were since I saw the scar on your knee when you were trying on the espadrilles. It confirmed what I'd begun to suspect. But if I hadn't known already, I should have guessed a moment ago when I was standing behind you. Almost everything about you is different, except for that little curved scar . . . and this.'

As he spoke, he traced with his fingertip a line from her temple to her chin. 'Even as a child you had this beautiful line here,' he said, his voice suddenly husky.

The next moment she was in his arms and he was kissing her, not gently as before, but fiercely, demanding a response.

Breathless, shaking, swept far from all her bearings by a wild hurricane of passion, Laurian leaned her hot forehead against Oliver's shoulder and felt the rapid beating of his heart against her hand, flat on his chest.

At first, when he picked her up and carried her to one of the capacious chintz-covered sofas, there to sit down with her on his knee, she was too overwhelmed to object. Even when he searched for and found the clasp of her fragile shell necklet and, having removed it and placed it safely on the end table, began to kiss her bare neck, she submitted in rapt, dazed silence.

It was not until when one of his hands paused close to her

own thudding heart and only a thin film of lace lay between his hard yachtsman's palm and the soft swell of her breast that she knew they were both in danger of losing control completely.

'Darling . . . stop . . . please . . . the party . . . your guests,' she murmured in broken gasps, the combination of having her neck kissed and her breast stroked being such an exquisite pleasure that she had difficulty in thinking or speaking.

'There are no guests,' he said thickly. 'The party is tomorrow. Tonight there is only us.'

Laurian opened her eyes. 'You mean you lied to me?'

Oliver stopped making love to her. Looking into her startled eyes, his own still bright with desire, he said, 'No, *I* didn't lie. Yours is the forked tongue, my darling. I merely made certain statements from which you drew false conclusions. If you haven't thrown my note away, re-read it. You'll see what I mean. Richard Lucas will be here . . . next week. Tonight we're strictly *à deux*.'

He bent to resume kissing her, but then thought of something and paused. 'It might be a wise precaution to lock the door . . . in case someone should wander in. Not likely but not impossible.'

Gently lifting her from his lap to the feather-filled cushions, he sprang up and crossed the room.

'You have lipstick all over your chin,' she said, as he turned towards her after locking the door. As he came nearer she jumped up, putting out her hands in a fending off gesture. 'Oliver, we must talk. If you knew who I was, why didn't you say so?'

'I was hoping you were going to tell me. Either way it didn't seem to matter much. We both knew the important thing—that we belonged together. At any rate I did. I knew it that day in London. If you hadn't turned up here, I was going back to find you. It wouldn't have been too difficult as you'd told me your occupation.'

'Are you saying it was love at first sight? I shouldn't have thought you'd believe in it.'

'I didn't—until it happened to me. I saw you come down the stairs in Hatchards and I thought "She's turned up—at last". I'd been beginning to think I was waiting for someone who didn't exist. Wasn't it the same for you?'

'Yes, it was,' Laurian confessed. 'Then you said who you were, and it was such a horrible shock. I was shattered. You see, I'd *hated* you . . . really loathed, despised and detested you. It was like . . . like the handsome prince suddenly turning into a beast, instead of the other way round. I didn't know what to do . . . so I walked out.'

'I should have chased after you, but I was a bit stunned myself,' he admitted, with a wry smile. 'It's disconcerting, to say the least, when a girl who's been looking at one with dove's eyes suddenly turns into a hostile virago. Rather stupidly, it didn't strike me that what had caused the transformation had been telling you my name. I thought of a dozen possible explanations—none of them holding water—before I hit on the correct one. What threw me off the right track was why, if you *were* little Laurie grown up, you hadn't known me on sight. You had changed out of all recognition. I hadn't.'

'When I knew you, you had a beard. It makes an enormous difference. And you weren't the suave man about town that you are today.'

He grinned at that. 'Makes me sound like what Archie used to call a bounder! Yes, I'd forgotten that beard I grew coming over.' He rubbed a hand over his jaw. 'It must have been damnably hot and uncomfortable once I got here.'

'Perhaps you were so unhappy, you didn't notice. Did Archie know about Judy? Did you tell him?' asked Laurian.

'I think so. I don't remember. It was a long time ago. Do you mind that I loved someone else in my salad days?'

'Oh, Oliver . . . *no!* Of course not. I just don't like to think of the pain you must have gone through.'

As she spoke, somewhere nearby a telephone started to ring.

'Who the devil is that?' he said, in a tone of annoyance. 'I said I wasn't to be disturbed this evening.' When it continued to ring, he shrugged and moved to answer it. 'Thornham here,' he said curtly.

Laurian was near enough to hear the apologetic tone of whoever was on the other end of the line, but after a moment she stopped listening, watching with loving wonder the frowning profile of the man who, it seemed, wanted her as much as she wanted him. Useless now—after those passionate kisses—to delude herself that she could ever live without him.

Oliver picked up the pencil lying beside the telephone pad. 'Yes, all right. Give me the number.' He wrote it down. 'Right: I'll pass that on to Miss Ford.'

Having rung off, he turned to her. 'Someone called Robert Adstock telephoned your hotel, wanting to speak to you as a matter or urgency. This is the number in England where you can reach him. I presume he's a close friend or colleague. He wouldn't say what he wanted; only that it was important and he must speak to you tonight.' He glanced at his watch. 'It's nearly midnight over there.'

For a little while Laurian had been in what old islanders called 'goat heaven' or 'kiddy kingdom', meaning a state of bliss. But while Oliver passed on the message, she had come back to earth with a bump.

She had no idea what Robert wanted; perhaps only to inform her that his father had died and he would now be involved in organising the funeral. But whatever the matter of urgency, afterwards she would have to explain his presence in her life to Oliver.

And whereas she could accept that he had once loved someone else, she was not sure of Oliver's reaction if he found out that, but for old Mr Adstock's sudden illness, she would not have been staying here alone.

CHAPTER FIVE

THERE WAS no delay in putting the call through to England. When the number was ringing. Oliver handed over the telephone and walked away to the other end of the room where he took a book at random from the shelves and sat down with it.

But although the library was a long room, Laurian knew he would not only be able to hear her side of the conversation but would probably listen to it as well. She could tell he wasn't pleased at having their rapprochement interrupted by another man, even though he didn't yet know Robert's position in her life.

She herself couldn't help feeling irritated. Surely nothing was so urgent that a message left for her and a call back first thing tomorrow wouldn't have sufficed? It wasn't as if Robert had been deeply attached to his father and would now be knocked sideways by grief. He had long grown away from his parents and visited them only from a reluctant sense of duty. It was sad, but it wasn't uncommon.

'Hello, Robert. It's Laurian,' she said, when he answered the telephone far away in the north of England.

'You always seem to be out when I ring up,' he said, without any preliminaries. 'Where are you now?'

'At another hotel. How are things with you?'

'Better. I'm flying out to join you tomorrow. I want you to meet me at the airport in Antigua tomorrow afternoon. It's only a short hop from you and then we can spend the evening together instead of my being there alone with nothing to do.'

In the light of what had happened in the past half-hour, this announcement left her speechless with shock and dismay.

'Laurian? Are you still there?'

'Yes . . . yes. I'm just . . . surprised. Yesterday you still sounded doubtful.'

'I've had a long talk with the consultant, and he thinks Dad's condition has stabilised now. My sister is here, don't forget, and if necessary I can get back pretty quickly.'

'Mm . . . but will you enjoy being away with the possibility of an urgent recall hanging over you?'

'You sound as if you don't want me to come,' he said sharply.

Laurian wondered what he would say if she admitted she didn't. But how could she say that to him when he had no idea how much her life had changed since their hurried parting at Heathrow? It was something she would have to break to him gradually, gently.

'It's a long way to come if you might be called back,' she replied. 'And it is awfully hot here. It takes most people several days to acclimatise. One woman at Emerald Beach sunbathed too long the first day and was badly burnt. Half an hour in the sun is the maximum for anyone with a fair skin.'

'Are you hinting that you don't like it there? I thought you were having a good time. You certainly don't sound as if you're at a loose end without me.'

'Well, I'm not. There's masses to do, and I'm lucky . . . I tan very quickly. Also I met the people I told you about, and now I've met someone else whom I knew years ago as a child.' As she said this she glanced at Oliver.

He was no longer idly skimming through the book but had returned it to its place and was scanning the rows of leather-bound volumes. He had his back to her and his hands in the pockets of his black dress trousers. She wondered what, if anything, he was making of this one-sided conversation.

Robert said, 'Whether you think it's a good idea or not, I'm coming out there. After the better part of a week up here, I'm ripe for a heart attack myself! It hasn't stopped raining since I got here and Mum's driving me scatty, going over and over what went wrong between me and Celie. I've told her about you . . . about us . . . but she doesn't want to know. Don't, for God's sake, tell me *you're* having second thoughts?'

She wanted to say, 'But nothing was settled between us', but she couldn't; not on the telephone and not with Oliver in the room.

Instead, she said, 'You certainly sound terribly uptight and frazzled. Perhaps a week of lotus-eating would be the best thing for you. All right: I'll be there to meet you. But you'd better call me again before your flight, in case of last-minute hitches. Try not to let your mother upset you, Robert. It isn't good for your blood pressure.'

After his last annual medical, he had been told that his blood pressure was on the high side for a man of his age. By the sound of things it must be even higher at the moment.

'The thought of seeing you before long will help me to keep calm,' he assured her. 'It seems for ever since we were together, Laurian. I've missed you every hour of every day. I don't suppose you've missed me if you've been enjoying yourself, but this week has proved to me how much I need you. I'll be able to tell you properly tomorrow night. There shouldn't be any problem about getting a flight to Antigua, should there?'

'I don't think so. I'll let you know when you call in the morning. This conversation must be costing the earth. We'd better say goodbye.'

'Goodbye, sweetheart. I can't wait to see you.'

'Till tomorrow, then . . . goodbye.'

Feeling that frazma was now an understatement for her present frame of mind, Laurian rang off, bracing herself to explain the situation to Oliver.

He was no longer looking at the books but was strolling towards her, his expression unexpectedly amused. 'Do I gather that some mother-fixated pansy from the world of fashion is about to descend upon us to stave off an incipient nervous breakdown?'

For a second or two she was baffled. Then it dawned on her that, to anyone listening to her remarks, this wasn't such a wild inference as it seemed at first thought. At some levels the rag trade and its ancillaries were known to include a lot of effeminate men, many of them with difficult mothers.

The thought of Robert's reaction to being taken for one of them was so funny that, worried as she was, she couldn't help laughing.

'I'm afraid your friend won't find me a sympathetic listener to his troubles,' said Oliver drily. 'Nor will you be. I want your undivided attention. He'll have to find friends of his own ilk. It shouldn't be difficult— there's a coterie here as everywhere.'

His tone held a good-natured tolerance for the human condition, in all its forms, which reminded Laurian strongly of Archie, the most charitable of men.

She was going to explain about Robert, but then Oliver asked, 'Are you hungry? Shall we start dinner . . . or at least have a drink?'

She hadn't noticed it before, but now she saw that, in a corner of the room, a table was laid for dinner *à deux* with candles waiting to be lit and a bottle of champagne in an ice bucket.

While Oliver was deftly removing the cage of gold wire from the cork, it came to her that it might be wiser not to correct his misapprehension about Robert. To talk about another man, to try to explain the circumstances which had led her to toy with the idea of marrying Robert, must spoil this romantic occasion, their first meal alone together.

Besides, there was so much else to talk about, so much she wanted to know about all that he had achieved here in the thirteen years since their lives had diverged.

'Shall I light the candles?' she suggested, seeing that a Palm Reef Club match-book had been left on the table for this purpose.

'If you would.' He was slowly easing the cork from the neck of the heavy bottle, allowing a wisp of effervescence to escape before he released it.

Laurian struck a match and touched it to the wicks of the two candles rising from circles of creamy hibiscus blossoms. As the twin flames added their golden glow to the other soft pools of light from wall sconces and table lamps, Oliver poured the gently frothing champagne into crystal flutes.

He handed one of them to her. Raising the other to toast her, he said, 'Welcome home, Laurian Bradford . . . soon, I hope, to become Laurian Thornham.'

The look in his eyes, the tenderness of his smile made her forget everything but her love for him.

'I'll drink to that very happily.' She circled his glass with hers and, moving closer, they sipped the wine with their arms linked. Then they kissed.

'You still have a smudge of lipstick on that aggressive chin,' she murmured, taking the handkerchief from her breast pocket to wipe away a faint smear of *Rose Clarinette*.

'Aggressive? Me? Not at all. I'm a peaceable man. I don't think I've lost my temper more than twice since you went away.'

'I'm glad I wasn't around when you did lose it. It bet it was worse than The Storm,' she teased.

Some of the very old islanders, to whom Archie had liked to chat when he went to town for provisions, could tell second-hand tales of the legendary hurricane of September 1898, known to their parents as The Storm.

'I seem to remember you throwing some pretty spectacular tantrums when Archie decided to send you to school,' Oliver reminded her. 'You blamed me for that decision, but in fact it was in his mind for some time before I arrived. I admit I encouraged the idea, but not to make your life miserable, as you thought at the time. I could see that, without some schooling, you would be a hopeless misfit.'

'Yes, I know. I realise that now. Although it wasn't until the other night, when you were telling the Bucklands how and why you arrived here, that I really began to see how much I'd misjudged you.'

As they disentangled their arms and he drew out a chair for her, she said, 'Oliver, that bear in your sitting-room . . . the teddy bear. Was he yours or Judy's?'

'It was hers. To her great disapproval, my bear went up in flames one Fireworks Night. She almost couldn't forgive me for that act of schoolboy callousness. She was an only child and had a big thing about her bear. After she died I couldn't throw it away. I thought I'd keep it for my children . . . if you don't mind?'

'How could I mind anything which has made you the person you are . . . the person I love?'

She reached across the table to touch his hand and, for the second time that evening, he kissed her fingers.

Presently, under the covers on the white porcelain bouillon bowls, they discovered a cold summer soup.

'This is *gazpacho*, isn't it?' said Laurian, recognising the flavour from a recent meal out with Robert at Martinez, a famous Spanish restaurant in London.

Oliver nodded. 'I like Spanish food. I was in northern Spain for a couple of days after we met in London. Have you been to Spain?'

She shook her head. 'Paris and New York are as far as I've travelled. Isn't Spain very touristy?'

'In parts. Not where I was. It's the same as the Caribbean; some parts are overcrowded, others remain comparatively unspoilt.'

When they had finished the *gazpacho*, he lifted the lid of a large covered silver dish to reveal a delectable-looking lobster salad. After that there were glasses of lemon syllabub, so that by the end of the meal Laurian's appetite was satisfied but she didn't feel she had eaten too much rich food.

'That was delicious,' she said, when Oliver suggested moving to one of the sofas for coffee.

'That menu is the one my chef prepares when American honeymooners come here and want to dine in private on their first night here. Unlike people from Europe, they don't arrive tired by a long flight and sated with airline food.'

'Surely most of your clientele must travel first class, don't they?'

'Yes, but the food still isn't comparable with ours and,

although they serve vegetarian and kosher dishes, I don't know of any airline which provides aphrodisiac menus for honeymooners—which is what we've just eaten.'

He gave her a caressing look before turning away to plug in an electric percolator not far from the low coffee table where two blue and gold *demi-tasses*, a dish of hand-made chocolates and a bottle of Williamine eau-de-vie were arranged on a lacquer tray.

Laurian found herself blushing. For the first time she wondered if he meant her to stay the night; took it for granted she would; had even arranged for a message to go to the Emerald Beach so that they wouldn't be concerned by her failure to return. Did she mind if he had?

Oliver sat down beside her, putting his arm round her waist and pulling her against his shoulder, but in a companionable way.

'If you still felt hostile towards me, why did you book a holiday near here?' he asked. 'Was it curiosity which brought you back?'

There had been moments when she had wondered if his friend Edgar Headley might have told him it hadn't been she who had booked her room and another, subsequently cancelled. Clearly he hadn't.

She snuggled against him, parrying the question with another. 'Weren't you ever curious about me?'

'Not very. I'm afraid that, having last seen you at an awkward stage of adolescence, it didn't occur to me that the next time we met I should be struck by a *coup de foudre*.' He put his lips to her temple and she felt them moving against her skin as he said, 'The portrait of you as a child is rather idealised . . . or perhaps it's fairer to say that it took an artist's eye to recognise your potential. I remember you as an untidy tomboy . . . all long bones and knobbly joints . . .

like a foal.' The hand at her waist moved upwards. 'None of these lovely curves.' He blew softly into her ear and then, with a gentle hand, turned her face up to his.

Laurian was roused by someone knocking on a door.

As she came awake—momentarily disorientated by finding she was not in her room at Emerald Beach—from outside the door a female voice with a West Indian accent announced that her breakfast was here.

Memory, blanked out by deep sleep, resumed its normal function, presenting her with instant and total recall of the events leading to her presence in a bedroom in one of the cottages in the grounds of the Palm Reef Club.

In a hurry she sat up, hastily piling the pillows behind her and pulling the sheet up under her armpits. 'Come in.'

The door to the sitting-room opened and a large dark-skinned woman in a short-sleeved pink dress entered the bedroom, balancing a large tray.

'Good mornin', ma'am. Did you sleep good?' she asked, with a smile.

'Yes, thank you. Like a log.'

The maid leaned over the wide bed and let down the legs of the tray so that it formed a bridge across Laurian's thighs.

'Mr Thornham, he always takes breakfast at six o'clock, don' matter what time he go to bed. He said to tell you he'll come by later . . . and he'll bring you some clothes, seein' as you wasn' plannin' on stayin' de night and don' have no other clothes but your pretty evenin' dress,' she said, as she straightened and stood by the bed, arms akimbo, 'I hear tell from Mr Thornham as how you was here at de Reef before he come?'

'Yes, I was. I was born here. Archibald Bradford was my

father.'

'Is dat so? Well, ain't dat amazin'?' Like the French, many West Indians had difficulty pronouncing the 'th' sound; and although educated people said 'this' and 'that', nearly all island people used 'de' for 'the'. 'So now you come back home to stay, nuh?'

The once familiar interrogative, tacked on to the end of most enquiries, made Laurian feel she had come home. At the same time the question worried her, because how could she come back? However, it was too soon after waking up to grapple with a problem of that order. She pushed it to the back of her mind.

'Perhaps . . . I'm not sure yet.'

The maid returned to the door where she paused to look back and say, 'I tell you somet'ing what is sure . . . Mr Thornham is one happy man since he set eyes on you, Mis' Bradford. Everyone will tell you de same—dat man's in goat heaven since you come.' Rolling her eyes and chuckling, she disappeared.

The guests here were certainly pampered in every way, thought Laurian, as she surveyed her breakfast tray. Laid with a pretty cloth, with a matching quilted coffee-pot cover, it bore all the hallmarks of *de luxe* catering; dewy rolls of butter in place of the ubiquitous foil-wrapped rectangles; thick-cut marmalade and fruity jam instead of mass-produced tubs of synthetic glob; a hot croissant wrapped in a napkin, wholemeal toast in a silver rack, fresh orange juice and two boiled eggs. In addition there was a glass of white wine and a velvety peach. Oliver also remembered Archie's dictum.

She had been having a shower and washing her hair when she heard his voice call, 'May I come in?'

Wrapped in a fluffy white bath sheet, monogrammed

PRC in pale blue satin-stitch, with a smaller towel wound round her head, she went through to the bedroom and saw him standing on the threshold of the other doorway, some clothing over his arm.

'Good morning. How are you?' he asked.

'In goat heaven . . . which is where you are, too, according to the maid who brought my breakfast. Does the whole place know about us?'

Olive tossed the things he was carrying on to the foot of the bed. 'If they don't, they soon will. Cloella has never been one to keep any gossip to herself.'

He crossed the room, picked Laurian up, whirled her round, set her down and gave her a vigorous kiss.

They had stayed up so late last night that, even though he had shaved before she arrived, by the time he kissed her goodnight his chin had been starting to prickle her softer complexion. His cheeks were now smooth again and she caught a faint pleasant whiff of some lemony lotion, or perhaps it was soap or shampoo.

'I have things to do—which perhaps is just as well,' he said, holding her away from him and looking down at her towel-wrapped body. 'I just looked in to say good morning and to bring you something to wear. When you're ready, come up to my sitting-room and we'll have coffee.'

He swung her round by the shoulders, pressed another warm kiss into the curve of her neck, gave her a playful spank on her rounded bottom and strode away to deal with whatever needed his attention.

He left Laurian feeling very happy, very much loved—until, with an unpleasant start as from a mild electric shock, she remembered that later today Robert was arriving and she had promised to meet him at Antigua airport.

'Oh, my goodness!' Wondering what time the flight to Antigua left—she felt sure there wasn't likely to be more than one a day—she began to bustle about to get herself dressed.

'The inter-island plane to Antigua leaves at ten-thirty, Miss Bradford,' said the hall porter on duty when Laurian had arrived in the main building by way of the reception lobby.

'Heavens! I'm not going to make it,' she exclaimed, aghast.

She had been woken at nine. Now it was ten, and to reach the airport from here would take all of forty minutes.

'Don't worry, ma'am. Mr Thornham will take you in his plane. He told me to call the airport and tell them to have it ready for take-off at noon. You'll be in Antigua in good time for lunch.'

'Oh . . . I didn't know he had a plane.'

'Yes, ma'am. Mr Thornham flies all over. He says it beats sailing.'

'I see . . . well, that's a relief. Thank you.' She mustered a smile and turned away. In one way it *was* a relief, but she also had an ominous feeling that it might mean she wouldn't get time to talk to Robert alone and explain about Oliver to him.

Walking slowly along the corridor towards the staircase, she told herself that perhaps she was worrying unnecessarily. It might be that Oliver had business on the other island which would occupy him while she was meeting her friend. She had no idea what kind of plane he flew, but if it were a small two-seater there wouldn't, surely, be room for them all and Robert's luggage?

Perhaps it was his intention to fly back alone, leaving them to stay overnight and follow him tomorrow. Travellers arriving from Europe by jumbo jet invariably made a one-night stop-over in Antigua; the flight times gave them no option.

Oliver wouldn't object to her staying overnight in a hotel with a man he assumed to be effeminate. But how would he feel about it when he discovered that Robert was as manly as he was?

Not quite as manly, actually, because Robert wasn't in such good shape; nor did he have Oliver's innate authority. But there was no difference between them in terms of sexual preference, although they might differ in their prowess as lovers. That was something Laurian would never know.

As they wouldn't be leaving the Reef until after eleven, and Oliver might still be busy, she decided to call on Mary Poole before going up to his room. The flowered shirt and white shorts he had brought to the cottage had come from Mary's shop, although at the time he had chosen them she had not yet come over from her house on the big island and might not yet know he had taken some of her stock.

There seemed to be no one about when Laurian walked into the attractive boutique with its racks of sun-clothes and swimsuits and displays of all the accessories a woman might want to add to her resort wardrobe.

She was looking at the price tag on a jungle print bikini when Mary emerged from the washroom.

'Oh . . . hello.' She looked startled at finding someone in the shop.

It was Laurian's immediate impression that Mary Poole had been crying. Then she blinked several times and explained, 'A small insect flew into my eye on the way here and I had trouble getting it out from under my eyelid.' She dabbed her left eye with a tissue. 'Is that shirt OK or would you like to change it? Oliver left me a note about it.'

'It's fine . . . I like it very much. I hear Richard Lucas will be staying here next week. Do you like his clothes? I do.'

'So do I. I've had one of his button-down Madras shirts for at least five years. The more faded it gets, the more I love the colours,' said Mary.

They passed an agreeable ten minutes exchanging opinions on clothes; agreeing that they both liked the subtle neutral colours used by Japanese designers but were less enthusiastic about their unstructured shapes and unflattering layers.

They would have continued chatting, but another woman came in to buy a bikini and Laurian left, still not wholly convinced that, in spite of her quick recovery, it had been an insect and not some private distress which Mary had been dealing with in the washroom.

At the top of the staircase she passed two young maids who returned her smile and then exchanged glances. When, on impulse, a few moments later Laurian looked over her shoulder, she found they had stopped to watch her instead of continuing on their way along the landing.

Their interest forced her to conclude that by now the entire staff knew their employer was romantically involved with a guest from the Emerald Beach who last night had had dinner with him in the library and later spent the night in one of the cottages.

What they were longing to know, no doubt, was where he had spent the night; with her, or in his own quarters.

From outside Oliver's sitting-room, she heard the staccato tapping of someone using a typewriter. She knocked lightly on the door and was bidden to enter.

Oliver was working at the table on the balcony, rattling away at great speed with his two index fingers.

'Make some coffee, would you, sweetie? Everything's there on the tray. You just have to plug in the kettle. I've almost finished these notes.'

It was as if they had never been separated, Laurian thought; as if her thirteen-year-old hero-worship had never turned to bitter disillusionment but had slowly and gradually matured into this strong grown-up love she felt sure would last all her life.

Presently, when he had finished his work and they were drinking coffee together in the sun, she said, 'Oliver, do you know of any reason why Mary should be upset? I was in her shop a little while ago and I think—but I can't be sure—that she might have been crying.'

Although he didn't take sugar, Oliver picked up his spoon and thoughtfully stirred his coffee. 'I should doubt it. Mary is a very level-headed person. Very little upsets her. One of the reasons she's popular is that she's never moody . . . and a calming influence when the girls on the staff get worked up about something.'

'Still, she has had a terrible tragedy in her life. She told me about her husband being killed in Ireland. She must think about that sometimes.'

'It might be that,' he agreed. 'I'll go down and have a word with her.'

'Don't let her know I said anything to you, will you? I could have been wrong.'

'Naturally not.' He checked the time by his watch. 'We'll meet in the lobby in twenty minutes. I need another kiss.' He drew her to her feet, folded his arms round her and kissed her eager mouth.

When he had gone, Laurian leaned on the balustrade, looking at the sea and remembering the acrimonious tone of her first conversation with him here. Soon, on the flight to

Antiqua, she would have to explain about Robert and possibly upset the sweet harmony they were enjoying at the moment. But it had to be done.

Oliver didn't mention Mary on the way across the sound to the Club's landing stage on the big island. Laurian guessed this was because they were being taken across by one of the mechanics from the marina.

Their road transport was an open-sided yellow mini-moke shaded by a gaily fringed yellow awning. As they set out on the road to St James which they had to pass to reach the airport, he said, 'I spent about ten minutes with Mary and couldn't see any sign that she wasn't her usual cheerful self. I think she would have told me if there'd been something on her mind. We've been friends for a long time. One of these days, I hope, she'll meet someone in need of a wife, whom she likes, and then we shall lose her.'

'Do you get many unattached men coming to the Club?' Laurian asked doubtfully.

'Oh, yes . . . quite a number of widowers on holiday with friends, or sometimes on their own.'

'Wouldn't most of them be too old for her?'

He took one hand off the wheel to reach out and stroke her bare leg. 'Let's not worry about Mary's matrimonial prospects today, huh? I'd rather talk about you. I told her your real name and asked if she knew of you as a designer, and she took me to task for my ignorance. I gather you've been hiding your light under a bushel. You're a big name and you've recently received a Design of the Year award, she tells me.'

Laurian nodded. 'It's amazing how far a woman of my age can go if she puts her mind to a career and has almost no social life and no distracting relationship with men.'

'None at all?' he asked, lifting an eyebrow.

'Not since my art school days, and then nothing serious.'

She was about to embark on the explanation of her relationship with Robert, when Oliver put in, 'On the whole, I think it's probably better if girls don't have serious relationships before their middle to late twenties. Most of them aren't fully mature before then. I remember Judy's parents were very much opposed to her taking off with me to New Zealand. They felt she was too young, and perhaps they were right.'

Far from minding this reference to the girl he had been going to marry, Laurian was glad she could now speak easily of her.

'Perhaps she was a girl whose métier would have been making a happy and comfortable home for her husband and children,' she suggested. 'Being a wife and mother *is* a career, and a demanding one—whatever the more aggressive feminists may say.'

Oliver made no comment on this because, a short distance ahead, two small boys were hopefully thumbing a lift.

'Do you mind if we pick up these scallywags?' he asked.

'Of course not.'

He brought the moke to a halt. 'Pile in, guys.'

'Tank you, suh.' 'Tank you very much, suh.' They scrambled in behind.

'Why aren't you two in school?'

For the rest of the way to town, the animated chatter of their passengers put a stop to serious conversations.

From a height of five hundred feet, every coral head and rock was clearly visible through the pellucid water which shaded from palest aquamarine at its shallowest to the colour of a peacock's neck where it was deep.

Gazing down from the passenger seat of Oliver's private

aeroplane, Laurian was enchanted. This was as thrilling an experience as the wonderful flying sequence in *Out of Africa*, and made all the more magical, as it had been for Karen Blixen in the film, by her bond with the pilot.

'That was fabulous, Oliver,' she told him, her face alight, when they had landed in Antigua.

'I'm glad you enjoyed it. The plan now is to have a swim, then lunch, then whatever we fancy until it's time to meet your friend's flight.'

'But I have nothing to swim in.'

'Yes, you have . . . and a towel to dry on and flip-flops to protect your feet when the sand gets too hot to walk on. It's all organised.'

Half an hour later, wearing the bikini she had looked at in Mary's shop, Laurian was running into the sea from the beach of one of Antigua's best hotels.

It was the first time, this time, that she had seen him without a shirt on. His torso was still as deeply bronzed and as lean round the ribs and as strongly muscled above them as it had been in his twenties. He reminded her of drawings by Rodin, whose sculpture *The Kiss*, a nude man and woman embracing, had caused a shocked outcry when it was first exhibited and now was seen to portray the most sublime tenderness.

Even when he was wearing nothing but a black slip which, judging by its brevity, must have come from one of the French islands, Oliver still didn't look like what Connie had called him—beefcake. His muscles were not the curiously grotesque result of deliberate body-building, but rather the natural consequence of many vigorous activities. Laurian had forgotten how well he swam, cleaving through the water with clean sweeping arm strokes, the scissor movements of his long legs adding their propulsion to his passage.

'You still swim like a fish. How come?' he asked, as they walked back to their towels, shining beads of moisture sliding down his brown-satin skin.

She told him about the indoor pool in London. 'A poor substitute for this, but better than nothing,' she added.

Apart from rough-towelling their hair, they let the sun dry them off, which it did in a matter of minutes.

'Want some gel on your back?' asked Oliver, producing a tube from the large unadorned straw bag in which he had packed his gear and hers.

'Yes, please.'

They had spread their towels over the plastic webbing on the hotel's sun-beds. Laurian lay face down and folded her arms to make a cushion for her head. She felt him untie the bow in the centre of her back and flick the strings out of the way before squeezing several inches of gel along the line of her spine. With long strokes of his fingertips he spread it over her skin, his touch feather-light.

Laurian had once had a facial but never a massage. She didn't like the idea of being touched in so intimate a way by someone of her own sex, still less by a masseur. She had once been accused by one of her art school boyfriends, when she had jibbed at going to a mixed sauna party, of having a serious hang-up. If she had ever had one, it wasn't operating now. The combination of the hot midday sun and Oliver's fingers smoothing the gel over her shoulders and then down over her hips to the edge of her bikini slip was, she found, intensely pleasurable, turning her thoughts to even more sensuous delights.

What had he meant about doing 'whatever we fancy' after lunch? She knew how she would like to spend the afternoon: with him, in a shuttered room, making love on a taut white sheet on a fan-cooled bed.

'Are you sleepy?' he asked.

She lifted her head from her arms and twisted it round to look at him. 'With you stroking me? Anything but!'

His eyes were narrowed against the brilliance of the light. She couldn't see his pupils.

'You didn't get to sleep till the small hours. You might feel like a siesta.' He leaned towards her to fasten the strings of her top. 'Roll over and I'll do your front.'

There was no one left on the beach now. Everyone who had been there when they arrived had gone up to the terrace for lunch. Where they were, close to the base of a high stone retaining wall with coral-coloured mesembryanthemums cascading over the top of it, no one could see them.

Laurian turned on her back, raising a forearm to shade her eyes from the dazzle. Squinting down, under her lashes, at the front of her body, she could see Oliver's hand holding the tube and squeezing the gel in a glistening ring round her navel. This time he used the heel of his hand to spread it around, and a stronger pressure than before which, with every firm stroke, made her nerve-ends twitch more convulsively.

Lying very still, scarcely breathing, she heard him say, 'Antigua is supposed to have a beach for every day of the year . . . some of them very secluded. Perhaps we can find one to ourselves.'

'Perhaps . . .' Her answer was a dry-throated whisper which merged with an indrawn gasp as he suddenly drew his short nails across the sleek skin of her belly.

'Oh, God!' She jack-knifed up, catching his hand between hers. 'You have no idea what that does to me!'

'Nor you what you do to me.' Oliver slid his free hand behind her neck and drew her face closer to press his mouth softly on hers. 'I think the sooner we get married the better. If I organise a special licence, how would your limp-wristed friend like to give you away?'

She drew back. 'Oliver, I must put you straight about Robert. There's nothing limp-wristed about him. He's as heterosexual as you are.'

He was visibly startled. 'If that's so, what's he doing coming out here to be with you?'

'We're very old friends. We have flats in the same house.' She explained how that had come about. Then, feeling that, now she had begun, it was better to be honest about the original arrangements, she went on to tell him how, but for old Mr Adstock's heart attack, they would have arrived at Emerald Beach together.

Oliver listened in silence. 'I see,' he said, when she had finished. He sounded so matter-of-fact that for a few moments she thought he had nothing more to say on the subject.

But he had. 'Is he in love with you?' he asked.

The pause before she answered was so infinitesimal that it wasn't even long enough for him to jump to the conclusion that her hesitation could be taken as an affirmative. Yet in that small space of time she saw—and tried not to see—that this new-found happiness had no stability. It was like a house built on quicksand.

'Robert needs *someone*,' she explained. 'He had a wife . . . now married to someone else. Being single doesn't suit him. He would have liked out friendship to develop into something closer. We've never been lovers.'

'But he's hoping that will change when he gets here?' Oliver said shrewdly.

'Hoping, perhaps . . . but not taking it for granted. I've

always held back from a *faute de mieux* relationship with him. I don't think life is about second bests . . . substitutes. It's better to save one's money and oneself for the best . . . the real thing. Only sometimes, with love, one wonders if it's ever going to happen . . . if it's just wishful thinking.'

To her relief, he nodded. 'I know what you mean. It's dangerously easy to settle for what's available whenever what one really wants is hard to come by or, apparently, non-existent. I've found that applies to everything . . . from something as mundane as a light fitting to the more crucial choices one has to make in life.'

Since they were on the subject, and she couldn't help being curious about that side of his life, Laurian remarked, 'You must have had a lot of opportunities to settle for available women. I'm sure you could have had a brief fling with Atalanta Buckland if you had wanted to.'

Oliver shrugged. 'She would probably be happy with Henry if he paid more attention to her. She spends all day relaxing, reading erotic books. He spends all day in the sea, tiring himself out. Later he had a good dinner and a lot of rum punches. By the time they go to bed, he's zonked out. One sees it all the time.'

He swung his legs on to his sun-bed and lay down, his hands linked at the back of his head. With still-damp hair, carelessly swept from his forehead by a couple of rakes with his fingers, he looked more like the Oliver she remembered and less like the debonair stranger who had made her heart stop in London.

She said, 'It isn't always the man's fault when a marriage doesn't work well.'

'Obviously not, and we see the reverse of the medal often enough . . . wives who chip away at their husbands' confidence, and so on. A hotel is a great vantage point for observing the frailties of human nature,' he said dryly.

'But now and again two people arrive at the Club who still want a double bed and go off for walks holding hands and whose general behaviour indicates they made a good choice in the first place and time has only increased the rapport between them.'

He had been looking at the sea, but now he switched his gaze to her face. 'That's the kind of marriage I want . . . and intend to have.'

Laurian knew this was the moment when she ought to say something about the place her work played in her life; how she couldn't just shelve it, adapting immediately and completely to the style of life he had built up.

But as she was choosing her words, he said, 'If Adstock doesn't know about me, you're going to have a lot of explaining to do when he steps off the plane and you introduce me as your future husband.'

'Perhaps it would be better if I broke it to him gently before he meets you.'

'While I kick my heels elsewhere? Not a chance,' he said firmly. 'You may underestimate his belief that this holiday together would work out the way he hoped. If, at the end of a tiring flight, he's confronted with a crushing disappointment, he may cut up rough. I'd rather he vented his feelings on me.'

'He isn't a hot-tempered person. Perhaps that's why I held off . . . because I always knew I would be the dominant partner,' she said thoughtfully. 'I don't want to be that . . . or to be totally dominated,' she added.

'Meaning you think I might try?' he asked, with a lifted eyebrow.

She smiled. 'Not really, but you did give a masterly impression of a thoroughly autocratic, overbearing male after I was caught trespassing!'

'Didn't you guess there was a personal reason for preventing you leaving behind the official one?'

'If I had, I'd have thought you were paying me out for giving you a public brush-off in Fortnum's.'

His fingers still interlaced, Oliver sat up; his hands coming apart and his elbows dropping at the same time that the muscles cladding his midriff pulled him smoothly into a sitting position. Seeing the ease of that fluid movement sent another responsive tremor through her.

It was almost frightening how, after years of not meeting anyone who attracted her, and never really responding to Robert's tentative kisses, she found herself constantly aware of Oliver's body, his hands, the mouth which last night in the library had kissed away every doubt that they were made for each other, and always had been.

'My ego is pretty resilient,' he said. 'Anyway, in London you could have slapped my face or socked me in the eye and it would have been no more than a five-minute wonder. Possibly someone there might have recognised you. No one knew me from Adam. Here, it's a different matter. I'm known and so will you be.'

'I doubt if many people remember that Ol' Man Bradford had a daughter.'

'A few will, and word will soon spread that you're going to be my wife. Several of our maids have "family" at Emerald Beach. When we get back you'll have to pack and move out. You can't stay where you are once Adstock arrives.'

'It seems rather hard on Robert to present him with you and then desert him. I must spend some time with him, Oliver. He will still be my friend—I hope!'

'He can come and see you at the Club. Shall we have

lunch now?'

They ate at a table by the pool where Oliver was recognised by the proprietor of the hotel, who invited himself to sit with them. He was an entertaining man who, when he discovered Laurian's profession, insisted on sending for his wife—they lived in a house in the grounds—who was what he described as 'a clothes fanatic'.

She was equally lively and amusing and, at any other time, Laurian would have enjoyed meeting them. Today she wanted to be alone with Oliver, either at the secluded beach he had spoken of earlier, or at least broaching the problem of how their lives could be melded.

He, however, showed no impatience to break up the foursome. It was mid-afternoon when he suggested another swim in the sea before they drove to the airport in the moke he had rented. That he no longer seemed impatient to be alone with her made Laurian wonder if he was more put out about Robert than he had let on.

Robert's reaction to Oliver, when he realised Laurian had someone with her, was barely concealed displeasure. To have explained Oliver to him would have been the last straw. She couldn't bring herself to do it, introducing him as a friend from childhood who had kindly flown her over in his plane.

'How was your flight?' she asked, when the two men had shaken hands.

'Bloody awful,' Robert said shortly. 'The first class was full, so I had to fly tourist . . . next to no leg room and a fidgeting kid in the next seat. God, it's hot here! I need a shower and a change of clothes. How far is it to the hotel?'

'You should be under the shower in a couple of hours,' Oliver told him.

'Two hours!' Robert expostulated. 'Where is the place,

for God's sake? I thought this was quite a small island.'

'It is, but we thought you'd prefer to get all the travelling over and done with, instead of having to come back here tomorrow morning for the commercial flight,' Laurian explained. 'It's also a much nicer trip by private plane.'

'Oh, I see.' Robert's frown cleared slightly, although he still looked tired and cross as Oliver organised a porter to wheel his baggage to the part of the airport used by small aircraft.

However, the short return flight, with him in the seat next to Oliver's and Laurian sitting behind, cheered him up when he saw below them the crystalline sea and the outlines of reefs like those which, first thing tomorrow, he would be able to start exploring.

When they had landed and were completing the journey in the yellow moke, Laurian was nervous in case Oliver said something to precipitate the explanation which she didn't want to begin until Robert had showered and changed and had a rum punch in his hand.

To her relief the conversation stayed on innocuous subjects such as property values in the Caribbean, how the island was run and the frequency of hurricanes.

It wasn't until they drew up outside the Emerald Beach Hotel, and the youth who dealt with the luggage came out to unload Robert's bags, that Oliver said, 'I won't come in for a drink as I know you're looking forward to a shower.'

He waited until they had both climbed out before he added, 'If you have dinner here, Laurian, it will give you plenty of time to put Robert in the picture. I'll come over and pick you up about half past nine. See you later, Adstock.'

With a nod and a wave, he drove away.

'What does he mean . . . put me in the picture?' asked

Robert. 'And why is he picking us up? I don't want to go out on the town tonight. I've been in transit all day—I'm bushed.'

'We're not going out on the town. I'll explain later . . . when you've settled in.'

Laurian's heart sank at the thought of hurting him. But it had to be done.

'You have to be joking!' he exclaimed incredulously.

They were in a corner of the restaurant, having an early supper, part of an elaborate buffet which the rest of the guests would eat later. Not having fancied the fare provided in tourist class, Robert had not had a meal since his breakfast in England and had been extremely hungry.

While Laurian was explaining how she had grown up near here he had continued to eat with unimpaired appetite. But for the past few minutes while she told him, as gently as possible, that she had fallen in love, he had listened to her in stunned silence, the food on his plate forgotten.

'I don't believe this. You must have a touch of the sun,' he expostulated now.

Laurian looked down at her cold chicken salad, which so far had stayed untouched although she had a fork in her hand. She wasn't in the least hungry but had pretended to be for his benefit.

'I can see this guy is good-looking and macho and all that,' said Robert. 'He probably turns on most women. But what else do you know about him? You have to *know* someone, Laurian, before you tie yourself to them.'

'I do know Oliver. I've known him since I was thirteen. He virtually lived with us for several months before I went away to school.'

'How often have you seen him since then?'

'Not at all, but——'

'Have you written to each other? How often? Once a month?'

'No, we haven't, but——'

'You've never ever mentioned Oliver Thornham. Or being born here. Or anything about this place. Why not?'

She poked at a piece of tomato. 'I should have thought it was obvious. I—I adored Archie. He was my only family. I was heartbroken when he died. It wasn't something I wanted to talk about.'

'That isn't good enough, Laurian,' Robert said sharply. 'There's more to it than that, isn't there? Your father's house on this offshore island you've mentioned . . . it wasn't left to you, is that right?'

'No, it was sold.'

'Who owns it now?'

'Oliver does. He bought it. The money paid for my education. For a while, I admit, there was a rift between us . . . at least on my side, but soon after I arrived here, I realised I had misjudged him. He's put up the most lovely plaque to my father's memory. He's rescued the place from the verge of ruin—as a child I didn't realise how run-down it was—and made a going concern of it.'

'What kind of going concern?'

'It's called the Palm Reef Club . . . it's an exclusive hotel with some private cottage accommodation and a marina for yachts which have booked a berth . . . not just any old yacht which happens along.'

'Sounds to me like a goldmine,' remarked Robert. 'But all the time you were in England this guy never made contact . . . never found out how you were doing . . . offered you financial help?'

'No . . . but I didn't need it. My education was covered

and all my other expenses till I was eighteen. Then I won the scholarship to art school and was able to earn some money of my own in the holidays.'

'You could have done with some help and you know it,' he told her. 'Anyway, even if Oliver Thornham hadn't been doing well for himself, it would have been common decency to keep in touch with you.'

'He did write at first, but I tore the letters up. I was angry with him because I thought it was his idea to have me sent to boarding school. I've since found out it wasn't.'

'OK, so you tore up his letters. Don't you think, in his shoes, that later on you'd have written again . . . perhaps come to see you? I presume he does go to England sometimes? Where do his parents live?'

'I don't know much about them.' Laurian remembered the photographs in Oliver's sitting-room. 'I think his mother died some time ago. His father may also be dead.'

'Has he brothers or sisters?'

'I don't know. He never used to talk about his background and since I came back there hasn't been time to discuss anything but how we feel about each other. Robert, I don't want to hurt you, but I can't help what's happened to me. What you and I had—and still have—was never a love affair. It was friendship . . . an affectionate friendship.'

'It was never love on your side. It was . . . *is* . . . on mine,' he said glumly. 'Not that I ever felt sure you might marry me—not until you agreed to this holiday. Then I began to feel more hopeful. God, if only I'd picked somewhere else to go! The Maldives . . . Phuket Island . . . Bali.' He slumped back in his chair and ran both hands down his face in a gesture of weary despair. 'If we'd gone somewhere else this wouldn't have happened . . . you wouldn't have remembered his existence.'

'It wouldn't have made any difference. I met him in London, the day before I flew out here. We ran into each other in Hatchards and had tea together . . . neither of us knowing who the other was, but both of us recognising someone important to us.'

'You let him pick you up?'

'Yes.'

'I don't understand why you didn't recognise him.'

Laurian explained about Oliver's beard and how much she had changed from the sea urchin he had known. She didn't tell him how she had walked out on Oliver; it didn't seem relevant now.

'I need another drink.' Robert snapped his fingers to attract the attention of the only waiter on duty, who was busy arranging cutlery on the long buffet table.

'You don' like salad, ma'am?' the young man asked, concerned at the sight of her plate.

'It's fine . . . I'm just not hungry this evening. Please apologise to the chef for me.'

Robert ordered coffee for them both and another rum punch for himself.

When the waiter had gone, he said, 'It's sweltering in here, even with the fans going. Would it be cooler outside?'

'If we go on to the terrace, people will start coming down for pre-dinner drinks and I'll have to introduce you.'

'I don't want to meet anyone tonight. Let's go up to my room or your room and sit on the balcony.'

While he was unpacking his case and taking a shower, she had been packing her things. Her case was now locked, ready to be brought down when Oliver came to fetch her.

'That would raise eyebrows, Robert. The reason Oliver is coming back later is that he feels I shouldn't go on staying here now that you've arrived. This isn't London where anything goes. The staff here notice and gossip about everything.'

Robert's face, markedly pale by comparison with everyone else's except those of other new arrivals, began to redden like a turkey-cock's wattles. She could almost see the pressure of anger building up inside him.

'Can't sit on a balcony together . . . can't sleep under the same roof . . . he's got a nerve!' he burst out. 'I bet he didn't lose any time rushing you into his bed. *Have* you let him make love to you?'

Laurian's topaz eyes sparkled and a flush tingled her golden tan, but her voice remained quiet as she said, 'Please don't lose your temper, Robert. It won't help to have a row.'

'I bet you have,' he said bitterly. 'Here's me been patiently waiting . . . glad to get the odd kiss . . . and that bastard has swept you off your feet——'

'I'm not going to stay if you're going to talk to me like that.' She was already on her feet.

'No . . . wait . . . I'm sorry, Laurie. Please . . . sit down again.'

Their coffee was coming. She sat down. There was an uncomfortable silence while the waiter arranged the cups, poured the coffee and replaced the empty punch glass with a full one.

Robert, brooding, ignored him. Laurian mustered a smile. 'Thank you.'

'You're welcome.' The staff used a lot of Americanisms.

When the waiter was out of earshot, Robert said, 'I'm sorry I lost my temper. I won't do it again. But it's been a shock. Coming on top of my time up north, plus the journey, it's rather knocked me sideways.'

'Yes, I understand that.'

Laurian sipped her coffee. He took a swig of rum punch. She hoped he realised how potent they were. Under cover of the table, she glanced furtively at her watch. There was almost an hour to wait before Oliver came, and even then the day's tensions wouldn't be over.

She had to ask him what Robert had asked her: *why* hadn't he kept in touch? Why, since it must be some years since the Club began to be profitable, had he never checked to make sure she didn't need financial help?

He had known she was alone in the world, Wasn't there something anomalous about raising a plaque to her father but never troubling to find out if Archie's child—and the portrait of Neptune's daughter should have been a reminder—was making her way in the world?

These were all questions she had thought of before Robert raised them; but had pushed to the back of her mind in case the answers didn't tally with her new view of Oliver.

She knew she couldn't go on ignoring them.

CHAPTER SIX

'WHERE'S ADSTOCK?' asked Oliver, finding Laurian waiting for him in the lobby, her suitcase already brought down and standing beside the sofa where she had been flicking through a magazine.

'He was tired out . . . he went to bed.'

Oliver picked up her case and carried it out to the moke. 'How did he take it?'

'He was shocked and upset. He thinks I'm mad . . . that we both are.'

'You look exhausted,' he said. 'You'd better turn in early too . . . catch up the sleep you lost last night.'

'I do feel tired,' she agreed.

Too tired to press for an explanation of the things which puzzled her. She would ask him about them tomorrow.

The headlamps lit up the trees at the side of the road; the great buttressed trunk of an eighty-foot silk cotton tree, many tamarinds, breadfruit trees with shiny green foliage, mangoes. She had never been on this road at night before. Illuminated by the powerful beams, the trees looked curiously illusory, like the painted flats of a stage set.

When, presently, the vegetation on the seaward side of the road thinned out, showing moon-silvered water and the black silhouettes of coconut palms, she was reminded of photographs in travel brochures. None of it seemed real. It would not have surprised her suddenly to wake up and find it had all been a dream, and she was back in her bedroom in

156

the house in Spitalfields with a busy day at *Laurian* ahead of her, and the islands of her childhood only a poignant memory.

Oliver drove the moke into the palm-thatched car port where it and the Club's other vehicles were under the guardianship of a family who lived across the road in a little wooden house painted banana yellow with a sky-blue trim.

'Did you eat any dinner?' he asked, on the way across the sound, this time with him at the tiller.

Laurian shook her head. 'It was too early for me.'

'And too fraught, no doubt,' he said dryly. 'Well, it's over now and done with. I shouldn't go on worrying about it. No one likes inflicting pain on other people, but sometimes it's unavoidable.'

She wondered if he spoke from experience; if, in the past thirteen years, there had been women with whom he had become involved, only to break it off with them when his interest waned. He had told Atalanta he had never played the field, but nor was he a monk.

'You don't know him,' Robert had said, before rum punch and fatigue had forced him to go to bed. 'You've had your head turned by a stranger . . . you can't deny it.'

'Oliver, when you used to go to Emerald Beach in the evening—the evenings you didn't spend with Archie and me—what did you do over there?' she asked. 'Drink rum? Dance with the tourists?'

If the question surprised him, he didn't show it. Nor did he hesitate before saying, 'I went over there to find out about running a hotel. Edgar Headley's predecessor used to let me pick his brains. I expect I knocked back a fair bit of rum in the process. I never danced—I was still missing Judy then.'

It was a straightforward, believable answer. Would his

answer to the other questions which fretted her be equally
direct, equally convincing?

'If you haven't eaten, you'd better have some chicken
sandwiches or perhaps an omelette,' he said. 'An empty
tummy will wake you up in the night. Is there anything you
fancy?'

'Some sandwiches will be fine.'

He himself carried her case to the cottage, ordering the
sandwiches on the way through the hotel.

Having placed her case on the rack in the bedroom, he
returned to the sitting-room, saying, 'The room-service
waiter should be along quite soon. I won't stay. A man who
used to come here with his wife, and is now on his own,
arrived here this afternoon. I think I should have a couple of
drinks with him. I'll see you tomorrow.'

He put his arms loosely round her, kissing her first on
one eyebrow, then on the other, and then, lightly, on her
mouth.

'Goodnight, my love. Sleep well.'

In the morning a different maid brought Laurian's
breakfast. Ther was an envelope on the tray addressed, in
Oliver's writing, to *Miss Bradford.*

Laurian hadn't slept well. During her wakeful periods
she had worried about today: facing him with those crucial
questions and seeing Robert again.

The note inside the envelope was brief and to the point.

A slight crisis during the night—visitor taken ill. The
hospital can probably cope, but her husband is inclined
to panic and may want her flown out. I may be tied up
all morning. Feel sure you can amuse yourself. O.

Again there was a glass of wine and a fresh peach on the

tray. But in place of boiled eggs there was kedgeree in a covered silver dish with hot water in the base of it.

Was this a coincidence, or had Oliver ordered it specially, remembering the kedgerees cooked by Archie in whose youth it had been a favourite breakfast dish in great country houses such as Kingscote Abbey!

As she ate it, she felt that what she ought to do this morning was to go back to Emerald Beach and see how Robert was faring. After some thought, she decided that if she could borrow a moke she would drive into St James to pick up the skirt she had ordered on her previous visit, delivering a note to Robert on the way there.

He was still her friend and the co-owner of the house. Oliver couldn't object to her lunching with him, on the way back from town. Robert would probably spend the morning snorkeling. That, after all, was the point of coming to the Caribbean.

There was no problem about borrowing a moke. The hall porter gave her the keys and the big man called Tiny took her over. There was a telephone link between the car port and the marina. When she returned, she would have only a short wait before someone came to fetch her.

Driving into town reminded her of the journeys made with Archie in his open Rolls-Royce, a 1907 Silver Ghost with wide running boards and huge mudguards, which he had bought from someone down on their luck on the French Riviera and had shipped to the West Indies, a typical act of flamboyant extravagance.

Where was it now? Perhaps in the collection of a rich American vintage car enthusiast, restored to its original opulence after the years of being garaged in a shack shared by hens and used as a pick-up for groceries. That was something else to ask Oliver.

She had parked the moke and was walking across town to the shop where a skirt she had liked was being copied for her in a different material, when she was hailed by Steven and Mona, the Canadians from Vancouver.

'This'll interest you, Laurian,' said Steve, opening a wallet of photographs he was carrying. 'I just had these developed. Do you recognise anyone?'

He handed her a snapshot of the lagoon at night taken from the terrace. Crossing the moon-glade was a boat with two people in it, a man and a woman in silhouette. Herself and Oliver.

'Have it, if you'd like to,' he offered. 'We can have another print made.'

'Thank you.'

'Will you join us for a Coke or something?' invited Mona. 'We're on our way to that outdoor café in the main street.'

Laurian felt she couldn't refuse. On the way to the café, she learnt that the Canadian couple had been involved in the crisis during the night. Their bedroom was next door to that of the woman who was ill, and her husband had sought their help rather than calling the switchboard.

'He was really panicked,' said Mona. 'He thought his wife was dying. Then Oliver Thornham appeared and calmed him down and organised a doctor and everything. That man is just *so* reassuring, isn't he, Steve? You feel, no matter what happened, he would know how to deal with it. But I guess I don't need to tell you that.' She smiled at Laurian, clearly hoping for some clarification of their relationship.

'I expect he and John Lynn, his manager, have had to cope with most contingencies since the Club opened,' said Laurian.

But it made her feel warm inside to hear Oliver praised.

Later, she had collected her skirt and was idly window-shopping when an elderly white woman, whom at first she didn't recognise, approached her.

'Excuse me for speaking to you, but there's something about you which reminds me of a little girl I used to know. Bradford . . . Laura Bradford, her name was.'

'How clever of you to recognise me after all this time, Mrs Yardley!'

As soon as the woman spoke, Laurian had remembered her. Millicent Yardley, widow of the minor civil servant who had been second in command of the public works department when the island was run by the British.

Long ago, Mrs Yardley had tried to convince Archie Bradford that his daughter ought to wear dresses and learn to play the piano. Laurian could remember a conversation, going home in the old Rolls-Royce.

'I can't stand Mrs Yardley. She smells funny.'

'Mothballs and lavender water, m'dear. She's lonely . . . a fish out of water. Can't get on with the locals—thinks of them as "the natives"—and has no resources to make her life bearable, poor creature. Try to be patient with her.'

Mrs Yardley still smelt of mothballs. She professed herself overjoyed to see 'little Laura' again. Reluctantly, Laurian found herself accompanying her to the small house near the town playing-fields to which Mrs Yardley had moved after the death of her husband. She had not returned to England, she confided, because she no longer had any relations there and it was easier to stay put, even though she had never cared for the island.

The house was full of knick-knacks. Dusting it must take hours, thought Laurian. It smelt strongly of the insecticide with which, Mrs Yardley confided, she always had a good spray round before going out.

'I can't abide creepy-crawlies,' she said, with a shudder. 'I
hadn't been out here a week when Frank killed a scorpion in
the bathroom.'

Laurian stayed with her longer than she had intended,
wrung with pity for the little woman's loneliness. What
would happen to her when she could no longer look after
herself? she wondered anxiously.

When, as lunch time approached, she said she must go,
Mrs Yardley, who up to that point had talked of nothing
but her feuds with her neighbours and of how everything
had gone downhill since the island gained its independence,
started to take an interest in her visitor's affairs.

'You'll have come back to see your poor father's grave, no
doubt? I thought you would, one of these days. You know
the place where you lived is now a club for millionaires? If I
see that man in the street, I cut him. He used to speak to
me, but he's given up now, I'm glad to say. He knows I
haven't forgotten if everyone else has.'

'Are you talking about Oliver Thornham?' asked
Laurian. 'Why don't you like him, Mrs Yardley?'

She was already on her feet. Now Millicent Yardley got up
and came close to her, clutching Laurian's bare sun-tanned
arm with her thin fingers. Mrs Yardley's skin wasn't brown
except for the liver spots of age on the backs of her hands.

'It's my belief that that man *drove* your father to drink
. . . *and* had something to do with his death,' she said, her
voice low and conspiratorial, as if she might be overheard.
'They said it was an accident . . . but was it? Look what the
Thornham man stood to gain. They say he's well on the
way to becoming a millionaire himself now. Very generous
he is, so I've heard. Contributes to all the good causes.
Conscience money, if you ask me.'

* * *

It was long past lunch time when Laurian drove back the
way she had come. She drove more slowly and carefully
than she had on the outward journey, knowing it would be
easy, and dangerous, to let her mind wander. Strangely, it
was only now, some time after the initial shock, that she was
beginning to feel its full impact.

At first she had felt surprisingly calm, making her escape
from Mrs Yardley's house and walking back to the centre of
town wondering if the old lady was slightly mad or if part of
her tale was true.

Not for an instant had Laurian believed any of her
accusations about Oliver. But why had he kept it from her
that Archie had drowned after falling out of a boat in which
an empty bottle of whisky had been found?

She had found out the facts at the office of the island's
newspaper where they had yellowing copies going back
years. She probably wouldn't have thought of looking up
the report of the inquest if Neal, the younger of Dr and Mrs
Lingfield's two sons, hadn't been a sub-editor on a paper in
the Midlands and, in his earlier twenties, a reporter who
had often covered inquests.

Archibald Bradford's death and the inquiry into it had
made front page headlines on an island where nothing
much happened. Oliver, the last person to see him alive,
had given evidence of identification and, questioned by the
coroner, had agreed that the deceased had been drinking
heavily for some time.

On the day of the accident—the empty boat and Archie's
body had both been found within a few hours of his
death—Oliver had spent the whole day at Emerald Beach
with friends who had come out from England for a holiday.
Which proved, if proof were needed, that Mrs Yardley's

suspicions were unfounded and libellous.

As she approached the Emerald Beach hotel, Laurian considered calling in, but felt that she couldn't face Robert at the moment. Earlier, realising he might worry if she failed to turn up at lunch time as she had said in her note that she would, she had telephoned the hotel and asked for him to be given a message that she had been detained in town and wasn't sure when she would see him. No one at the Club would be worrying about her. She had told the hall porter she might not return until late afternoon.

She arrived at the Club's car port just as a boat brought some people ashore, so she didn't have to use the telephone link. On arriving at the reception desk, she asked, 'Has Mr Thornham returned now?'

'Yes, Miss Bradford, but he has someone with him at present. Shall I let him know you're back?'

'No, don't bother him if he's busy. I'll see him later.'

At the cottage, she had a shower and put on a clean top and shorts. Then she sat on the small veranda, looking out at the glittering sea and thinking of darling Archie taking a boat out, getting 'sozzled' as he called it, and falling into the water. If he hadn't taken to the bottle, he might still be alive, even though in his late eighties by now.

Why had he taken to drinking heavily? Because he missed her? Because he regretted selling the island to finance her education?

Tears filled her eyes and slid unregarded down her cheeks. What did an education, a career, success and fame matter compared with all they had both lost by being separated? Even if he had died of natural causes by now, they would have had more years together; more deep sea fishing trips, more barbecues on the beach, more jokes, more discussions, more hugs . . . more of the only thing which mattered in life. Giving and receiving love.

'Anyone at home?'

The woman's voice came from the path which, forking from one of the main pathways through the grounds, led only to the entrance to this cottage, approaching it from behind to give the occupants maximum privacy.

Laurian barely had time to wipe her wet cheeks with her fingers before Atalanta Buckland came into view.

'I rang your hotel to find out if you'd care to go shopping with me and was told you'd moved over here,' she said. 'Not that we've seen anything of you. I gather the big romance, which was clearly in the offing the night you and Oliver had dinner with us, is now in full flood. I rather envy you—he's incredibly attractive. He isn't here now, is he?' Her eyes went to the opening door leading directly into the sitting-room.

'No, I'm alone,' said Laurian, wishing she had heard Atalanta coming in time to disappear.

Her voice was husky and not quite under control, making Atalanta take off her sun-glasses to peer at her more closely.

'You've been crying, Oh, lord, have you had the first lovers' tiff? Or have you found out about the Poole woman? She hasn't been giving you hell for pinching her chap, has she? She doesn't look the termagant type. But hell hath no fury like a woman scorned, or a mistress discarded, so one hears.'

Laurian said nothing. How many more shocks was today going to spring?

Atalanta sat down, the folds of her beach wrap falling away from her brown legs. She crossed them.

'I was told about it by someone who's been coming here for years,' she explained. 'Until you arrived on the scene and broke it up, Oliver and Mary Poole had been having a very discreet affair for ages. But I shouldn't let it upset you. I don't suppose he's in love with her. She looks rather dull. I expect he just found her convenient. She has her own house quite near here, apparently.'

'Are you sure you can believe all you hear?' Laurian asked stiffly. 'If they're so discreet, how did your informant find out?'

'By looking through her husband's binoculars from the deck of their yacht. Mrs Poole's house isn't visible from the road, but it is from the sea. She saw them together in the garden. It has a small swimming pool, and they were both in the nude. I'd call that conclusive, wouldn't you?'

As she had, a short time ago, while thinking about Archie's end, Laurian felt pain inside her. Her heart ached for Mary Poole who she felt sure would never have embarked on an affair unless there was love on her side. Obviously she *had* been crying before she came out of the washroom yesterday morning; and later, Oliver, stirring his sugarless coffee, must have guessed why. He must also have been thinking of Mary when he told Laurian, last night, that no one liked inflicting pain but sometimes it was unavoidable.

'I think whoever told you that would have done better to keep it to herself,' she answered. 'I can't see the point of violating other people's privacy, which is what gossiping is. Did it really give her a kick to regale you with that particular titbit? If it did, she must be a very silly person.'

'I don't know what it did for her; it certainly brightened my day,' said the other woman, unabashed. 'Who would have imagined Mary Poole—a health foods and good deeds person if ever I saw one—cavorting without a stitch on with the macho Oliver? What's he like in bed? As good as one would hope?'

The casual effrontery of the question took Laurian's breath away. Her cheeks burned even redder than they had when Robert had asked her a not dissimilar question.

'I have no idea,' she retorted.

Atalanta roared with laughter. 'Then why are you occupying this love nest instead of staying where you were? Of course you're sleeping together, and jolly good luck to you. I only wish I were in your shoes . . . free as air with a super new lover. Take it from me, husbands get awfully boring after a while . . . sometimes even before the honeymoon is over,' she added, with a wry little grimace.

As she finished speaking, they both heard the firm, widely-spaced tread of a tall man in leather-soled shoes approaching the cottage.

'Who have we here, I wonder?' murmured Atalanta, with a naughty giggle.

A few moments later Oliver came round the corner of the building. When he saw who was Laurian, he didn't trouble to hide the fact that he would have preferred to find her alone.

'Good afternoon, Lady Henry,' he said, reverting to formality. 'I wonder if you would mind postponing your chat with Laurian. I have something private to discuss with her.'

Atalanta jumped up. 'I'm on my way.' She glanced at Laurian, her eyes bright with amusement. 'Such urgency!' Laughing, she went away.

Oliver showed neither curiosity or interest in the reason for her amusement or the meaning of her parting shot.

'Now she'll rush off and spread *that* titbit around,' said Laurian, biting her lip. 'Considering how discreet you've been in the past, you don't seem at all concerned to protect *my* reputation.'

The barbed remark was prompted by a mixture of stresses; she had suffered one devastating and one lesser shock, she still had Robert on her mind, and now they had come to the point when all her doubts and uncertainties about the past and the future could be put aside no longer but had to be tackled forthwith.

As if she hadn't spoken, Oliver looked sternly at her. 'Robert Adstock has been here, trying to convince me that you and I have no future together. He doesn't paint the same picture of your relationship that you did. Why did you lie to me, Laurian?'

'Lie to you? What about?'

'You specifically said you and he had never been lovers. I didn't ask—you volunteered that information. It makes no difference to me that you've had a close relationship with another man. You're not an immature girl and your past is your own affair. It *does* matter to me that you lied to me. I can't stand deliberate dishonesty.'

'Are you saying Robert told you we *were* lovers?' asked Laurian stiffly.

'Yes.'

'And you take his word before mine?'

'He doesn't strike me as a man who would make up something like that. It's obvious that his feelings towards you are very much stronger than you led me to believe. He's distraught at the prospect of losing you.'

'He must be, to tell you something which is completely untrue. Why should I lie about it? As you say, my past, if I had one, would be my business—unlike yours which seems to be everyone's business,' she flared at him.

Oliver's mouth hardened. 'What do you mean by that statement?'

'When Atalanta descended on me without warning, she

could see I was upset. She assumed I'd just found out about your . . . liaison with Mary Poole. She'd been told about it by someone else . . . someone who, from a boat, saw you sunbathing in Mrs Poole's garden. She wasn't wearing a swimsuit and neither were you.'

Oliver took it calmly, looking neither put out, embarrassed nor angry.

'I'm sorry you had to hear about it from that woman,' he said quietly. 'It's true that for a long time Mary and I were "close friends" as the newspapers put it. It wasn't a love affair and would never have led to marriage. We're very fond of each other and, I hope, always will be. Anything more is over and done with.'

'It can't have been over very long. I'm sure it was that she was crying about yesterday morning. Don't you think it was rather unfeeling—to say the least—to install me here in this cottage and let the staff know, as they obviously do, that you and I are involved now?'

'There was no other option,' he said. 'You couldn't have stayed where you were. There are no other first-rate hotels on this side of the island, and anyway you belong here. Mary told me, and I believed her, that she *was* crying yesterday, but not over me; over Tim, her husband. It would have been his birthday. She still longs for him. I was never more than a poor substitute for him. The fact that I'd been through a similar experience, years ago, made her feel more comfortable with me than with most people. That's how it started. She always knew it must come to an end eventually.'

For you. Not necessarily for her, she thought. Loving him, Laurian couldn't believe that the other woman's need for solace hadn't developed into a deeper feeling for him. She suspected the late Tim Poole's birthday had been a spur-of-the-moment explanation Mary had made up to spare Oliver the unease of knowing he had made her unhappy.

'You say you were upset before Lady Henry came here to spread the gossip. Why was that?' he asked.

'I was going to have lunch with Robert today. Did he tell you that?'

'Yes. You'd telephoned a message that you'd been detained in town. He didn't know why.'

Laurian folded her arms round her body as if she were cold. 'I met someone in St James who told me about Archie's accident. I went to the newspaper office and looked it up in their files.' Her eyes glazed with quick hot tears. 'If I'd been here it would never have happened. He wouldn't have started drinking . . . there wouldn't have been an accident.'

She gave a low moan of anguish, her eyes tightly closed but the tears seeping through her lashes.

Strong hands drew her to her feet. Comforting arms enclosed her. Everything else forgotten, she buried her face in Oliver's shoulder and wept.

It seemed a long time later that, stroking her hair, he said quietly, 'It wasn't an accident, my love. It was Archie's chosen way out. He was almost seventy-seven. He was incurably ill . . . had already had a lot of pain. He wanted to finish it quickly . . . not in hospital, doped to the eyeballs. He thought it might not be an end but a new beginning. He'd had a lot of fun in his life and he was ready to find out what might happen next.'

She drew back to look up at his face. 'It was suicide? How do you know? Did he leave a note? Did he *tell* you he was going to do it?'

'No. He wouldn't have burdened me with knowing and possibly feeling, later, that I should have stopped him. In fact I believe what he did was the right and sensible thing in the circumstances. You will too, when you've thought about it. The reason I know it wasn't an accident was that the night before he was reading Livy's history of the conflict between Rome and Carthage. You remember Hannibal, the Carthaginian general, was one of Archie's heroes?'

Laurian nodded, already guessing what he might be going to tell her.

'I found the book by his bed, several days later, after the inquest was over,' said Oliver. 'I was going to put it away when I noticed he'd scribbled my name on the cardboard bookmark he'd left in it. The page he had marked dealt with Hannibal's last years, always in exile, with a price on his head. Finally, when he was in the kingdom of Bythinia, Rome demanded that he be given up. They sent soldiers to take him, but Hannibal poisoned himself before they reached him. I knew it was Archie's way of telling me what had really happened; but I couldn't see any point in informing the coroner.'

She gave a long gusty sigh. 'I see. Somehow, if it was deliberate, it isn't so bad. I couldn't bear to think of him dying so horribly ignominiously . . . drunk . . . floundering . . . perhaps trying to get back inboard.' She shuddered at the scene which had been lurking in her imagination all afternoon.

'It wouldn't have been like that, darling.' Oliver's arms tightened round her, drawing her head back into the hollow of his shoulder. 'The bottle was more than half empty when he brought it downstairs that morning. On what was left in it, with Archie's head for liquor, he would have been more than capable of lowering himself over the side, perhaps having one final float with the sun on his face—you know how he loved that—and then . . . letting the sea end his pain. He wouldn't have been afraid.'

His words blotted out the horror seen in her mind's eye, replacing it with a vision of an old and wise man choosing to end his life in a way he preferred to a long, slow ordeal in bed.

Presently Oliver said, 'What you need is a cup of tea—and something to eat if you missed lunch. While I call room service, you go and wash your face. It will make you feel better.'

When she rejoined him on the veranda, she asked, 'How is that poor woman who was taken ill?'

'She's going to be fine. It wasn't as serious as it seemed.'

'You must be tired if you were up half the night.'

'I can manage without much sleep.'

A waiter arrived with a pot of tea, an avocado salad and a basket of the crusty rolls which were baked in the kitchens twice a day, Oliver had told her.

'What did you say to Robert?' she asked, when they were alone again.

'I said I was sorry for him—as I am—but there was nothing to be done about it. He disagreed. He thinks that, whatever we may feel for each other, our lives are too disparate to make a workable marriage. Whereas, according to him, you and he have everything in common, including the house in London you alrady share.'

'We have separate flats in the same building. Do you still believe he was telling you the truth and I wasn't?'

'No, not now. I'm sorry I doubted you, even for an hour or two.'

'How can we help having doubts when we've known each other short time?' she replied. 'The other time hardly counts. I still have doubts about you. There are things I must ask you, Oliver.'

'Ask away.'

'Why didn't you keep in touch with me? You must have known that, eventually, my hatred of you would die down. How could you cut me out of your life . . . forget me . . . especially when you were living on what should have been my island?'

'I didn't,' he said. 'Not completely. Seeing the place as it is now—running like clockwork, fashionable, profitable—I don't think you can conceive what an uphill struggle it was. Your father sold it to me for a song. But he only did that because he had a very clear idea of what he wanted to happen here. He could have sold it for much more, but then the future of the island would have been out of his hands, and once developers get hold of a property some pretty abominable things can happen to it.'

'I know. My own lovely house in Spitalfields was almost demolished to make way for an abomination,' said Laurian, with feeling.

'For the first five years after you left, I had to work my guts out,' Oliver went on. 'I had a colossal loan to pay off—the interest alone would have given me sleepless nights if I hadn't been too tired to think about it—and there were times when it seemed I was going to end up spectacularly bankrupt. Then I had an equally colossal piece of luck. There has to be luck in any successful venture. Mine was that a yacht came by with a party of some extremely influential Americans on board. The spread the word that this was a special place, and from there on I was sailing downhill.'

He broke off to refill their cups and to take a roll from the basket and borrow her knife to butter it.

'Up to that time I couldn't afford the time or the money

to come to Europe. As soon as I could, I did. I went up to Yorkshire to see you—and got a very cool reception from Dr and Mrs Lingfield. They said you were well and happy, that dredging up the past could only make you *un*happy, and suggested that I'd be doing you a service by staying out of your life.'

'I can't believe it. Why didn't they tell me?' Laurian exclaimed.

Oliver shrugged. 'Presumably because they thought it was in your best interests not to. Whatever they felt about me, my impression of them was favourable. Even so, I took the precaution of having them and you checked out. The report, by a professional investigator, confirmed that you'd been unofficially adopted by a thoroughly nice family, and were well on the way to achieving what Archie had wanted for you—independence.'

'All the same, I think it was wrong for them to conceal your visit.'

'You think that *now*. At the time it might have upset you.'

She thought about that for a moment. Perhaps he was right. After all, when they *had* met again, it had not been an auspicious encounter.

'So then you got on with your life and did forget me?' she said.

'Except for the odd fleeting thought—yes, I did.'

'And I forgot you,' she said, leaning back in her chair. 'And I'm not sure fate has been kind to throw us together again. Robert may be right. How can it work when we don't even function on the same side of the Atlantic?'

Three days later Laurian sat in the back of a taxi taking her to the airport on the first short lap of her journey back to London. She had the lowering feeling she might never come back, might never see Oliver again.

He was now in Barbados, attending an important conference of delegates from all the islands in the eastern Caribbean who were meeting to discuss common problems of conservation. He had wanted her to go with him, but she had refused, seeing in his absence an opportunity to slip away without a heartrending farewell. It had been bad enough saying goodbye for, as he thought, two days. Their last embrace at the airport yesterday had left her in tears, although she had kept them at bay until he had gone.

She had not said goodbye to Robert, but left him a letter, explaining that she wanted to fly back alone and would be going up to Yorkshire to stay with the Lingfields for the rest of her holiday.

She arrived at the airport early, with time to kill before the flight to Antigua took off. The long haul across the Atlantic began late at night, arriving at Heathrow about mid-morning, local time. She could be in Yorkshire by tea-time. She still couldn't understand why her foster-parents had, in effect, closed the door in Oliver's face. It bothered her.

She was having a cup of tea in the airport's small cafeteria when she was startled to see Mary Poole looking, in an anxious searching way, around the main waiting area. Instantly Laurian thought something bad must have happened to Oliver. Her blood seemed to freeze in her veins, then she jumped up and rushed towards Mary.

'Are you looking for me? Is anything wrong?'

'Oh . . . there you are. Yes, I was. No, nothing's wrong. But I just found out you were leaving and I have to talk to you.'

'I've left my bag in there. We'd better go back to my table. Would you like a coffee?'

'No, no—there isn't much time and I have a lot to say. Are you going away because of me?'

Laurian shook her head. 'I know about you and Oliver . . . but that has nothing to do with my leaving. I just can't see any way he and I can make our lives fit together. I'm going back to London to think about it; but I have people there depending on me in the same way that he does here. More so, in my case, because he has an efficient manager who could run things. If I go, the whole shebang collapses.'

Mary sat down at the table. 'I can see that you can't desert them, especially at a time when jobs are in short supply. But couldn't you find someone else to take over everything but the actual designing? Must you be there all the time?'

Laurian gave her a curious look. 'I should have thought you'd be delighted to see the back of me.'

Mary shook her head. 'Oliver is in love with you. I've had love. I want him to have it.'

'Don't you love him?'

'Of course . . . but you're the one he wants. Besides, I can never give him children. He wouldn't have minded, if he'd loved me, but he doesn't. He's a wonderful man . . . kind, generous, strong in every way, morally as well as physically. You're a fool if you let him go because of your career. It's women who have to bend to the wind. They always have and they always will.'

This time it was Laurian who shook her head. 'Not any more, Mary. I know myself well enough to realise that, at twenty-six, I can't change and become a different kind of woman. It isn't only that other people depend on me. I've struggled to get where I am and I want to hang on to my achievements and build on them. I also want to spend my life with Oliver. I want it desperately.' She fiddled with the teaspoon. 'It's an impossible choice, and there doesn't seem to be any practicable compromise.'

'Oliver is going to be more than upset when he gets back and finds you gone. I take it you've left a letter for him?'

'Of course.' Laurian looked across the table at her. 'It was good of you to chase after me when you have every right to dislike and resent me.'

Mary gave her a twisted smile. 'There's nothing to dislike about you, my dear, and I always knew I was asking for heartache eventually.' After a pause, she added, 'Some time ago the owner of a chain of resort-wear shops in Florida offered me a job over there any time I felt like a change. I'm thinking of following that up. Is there any possibility that you could develop the boutique at the Club into a more ambitious business? There's no shortage of clever seamstresses here.'

'I've already thought about that, but no—it isn't the answer. I can't leave Europe. It's as simple as that.'

Mary nodded, 'I guess so,' she murmured, echoing the phrase used by many of her customers. 'Anyway, I shall be moving on soon. The Caribbean is most people's dream of heaven, but even paradise becomes monotonous after a while. Variety *is* the spice of life, one discovers.'

At that moment Laurian's flight was called.

Twenty-four hours later she was in the train to York where, in response to a telephone call from London, Mrs Lingfield would be waiting to meet her when she arrived.

England was enjoying an Indian summer, so the contrast between the golden light of the West Indies and the paler late autumn sunshine bathing the countryside of her adopted homeland wasn't as great as she had anticipated. But the grey clouds and rain-washed window-panes she had expected would have been more in keeping with the climate in her heart.

'How beautifully brown you are, lovie,' said her foster-mother, after they had hugged each other. 'But we weren't expecting you back yet. Where's Robert? In London?'

On the postcard Laurian had sent them soon after her arrival—if it had arrived before her—she hadn't mentioned that he had been detained at the last moment.

'No, he's still on holiday. Things didn't work out quite as planned, Ma.'

'Oh, dear,' said Barbara Lingfield, but being a woman of tact she didn't immediately ask what had gone wrong.

That the postcard hadn't come yet was made clear on the drive out of York when, once clear of the city traffic, she said, 'We had the whole family at home last weekend, which was fun. We were all betting twenty-five pence on where you and Robert were. I stand to win one pound fifty if you fetched up in the Seychelles,' she told Laurian, with a smiling glance.

'Sorry: you were miles out. Where did the others think we were?'

'Bill thought Crete, David's money was on the Maldives, Neal said Jamaica and Jenny and Susie voted for Bali and Tobago.'

'Everyone was wrong,' said Laurian. Knowing the correct answer was bound to come as a shock, and not wishing to startle Mrs Lingfield while she was driving, she softened the impact by saying, 'Susie was the closest with Tobago.'

'Oh . . . the Caribbean. Did Robert know you grew up in that part of the world?'

'No, he didn't. If he had, he probably wouldn't have chosen a hotel quite close to where I was born.'

'Oh, my dear—' The road being clear, Barbara Lingfield

took a hand off the wheel to touch Laurian's arm. 'Did it upset you going back there? Is that why you've come home before him?'

'Not really. I've fallen in love—with someone else. With Oliver Thornham, as a matter of fact.'

'Laurian . . . no! You haven't? Oh, my goodness, what a disaster!' Mrs Lingfield exclaimed distressfully. 'Of *all* the places to take you . . . where you were almost certain to run into the Thornham man!'

'You've met him, haven't you?' said Laurian.

Her foster-mother shot another glance at her. 'Obviously he's told you that he turned up here once and we didn't exactly make him welcome.'

'He said you felt it would upset me to meet him.'

'Unquestionably it would have upset you . . . but apart from your deep dislike of him, we didn't take to him either.'

'Why not?' asked Laurian, curious to find out how anyone could resist Oliver's charm.

'He was rather too good to be true . . . very bronzed and attractive, very charming, I give you that. But a little too suave for his age, a trifle too sure of himself. Bill didn't trust him and neither did I.'

'I would trust him with my life,' Laurian assured her.

'But, my dear, you've only just met him. When you knew him before, you loathed him. You hadn't a good word to say for him.'

'I blamed him for sending me here, but it was my father's idea. Obviously my dislike of Oliver must have prejudiced you against him. He *is* almost too good to be true; but there's nothing spurious about him. Everyone likes and admires him.'

'What does Robert think of him?' her foster-mother asked drily.

'I'm sure he'd like him as well . . . in other circumstances.'

'If, as you say, you're in love with him, why are you here and not there? Or is he in England too?'

'No, he's still in the Caribbean. In a manner of speaking, I ran away,' said Laurian. Looking out at the familiar landscape of woods and fields as they approached the village near her boarding school, she explained her dilemma to Mrs Lingfield.

Later that evening, after Dr Lingfield had come back from evening surgery at the modern clinic he shared with three other GPs, and while fifteen-year-old Susie was upstairs, busy with homework, her foster-parents tried to persuade Laurian that what she felt for Oliver was an infatuation, not an enduring love.

As she listened to their loving advice she saw, as never before, how restricted their lives had been. Brought up near where they lived now, married before Pa had qualified, entirely content with a placid existence which had never taken them further south than London for Bill's medical and Barbara's musical training, or further north than the west coast of Scotland where they always spent their holidays, the Lingfields were as happy and settled a couple as it was possible to find.

Oliver's unexpected advent must have been as disturbing as a wild hawk's arrival in a hen run. They wouldn't have liked Archie either, she realised, had they known him. To their conventional eyes, he would have seemed eccentric, even raffish.

'There's something I think you should know, Laurie,' said the doctor, seeing they had failed to convince her of the basic unwisdom of her feelings, never mind the problems attaching to them. 'It may be that Thornham has an ulterior motive for making a set at you.'

'What do you mean, Pa? How could he have an ulterior motive?'

'From what you tell us about this Palm Reef Club, it must be an extremely valuable property, worth goodness knows how many millions of dollars now.'

'Yes, it must be,' Laurian agreed.

'He doesn't own it outright,' said Barbara Lingfield. 'When we told him we thought you ought to have some share in the proceeds of the venture, he said he would do what he could if you were ever in serious need of financial help, but it was your father's wish that you made your own way in the world. He also said that, if you have a son, the island passes to him . . . Archibald Bradford's grandson.'

'And Thornham may feel,' put in her husband, 'that it would be no great hardship to make sure your father's grandson is also his son. Do you follow me?'

Before Laurian could answer, her foster-mother put in, 'Perhaps you already knew that . . . perhaps he explained that provision to you?'

'No, it wasn't mentioned. But as he told you, years ago, he may have assumed I knew. I'm sure it has nothing to do with his wanting to marry me.' But even as she spoke, she remembered telling Oliver that his visit had been kept secret from her.

The telephone rang. As Dr Lingfield wasn't on night duty, it had to be a private call. All the time she had been in the house, Laurian had been hoping that Oliver, who by now must be back from Barbados, would ring up demanding to know why she had run out on him.

But by the time she went to bed there had been no call from him.

Having intended to stay in Yorkshire for several days, the next day she went back to London.

The Lingfields' house, for so long a haven, and the Lingfields themselves, until recently second only to Archie in her affections, no longer offered a refuge from life and its difficulties. If she hadn't known it before, she was learning rapidly that, for a woman in love, there was only one refuge from trouble—in the arms of her lover.

By the time she had been back in England for thirty-six hours, Laurian felt she was being torn in two by the demands of her career and her desperate longing for Oliver. Half a dozen times she had been tempted to call him, but each time she had resisted the compulsion to hear his voice. As he hadn't called her, he might be too angry to speak to her.

On the evening of her second day back, passing from her kitchen to her sitting-room, close to the door to the staircase, she thought she heard from below the rattle of a key in the front door of the house. Thinking it must be Robert, back ahead of time, she put down what she was carrying and went to investigate.

'Oliver!'

Looking down over the banisters, from the top of the first flight of stairs, she could hardly believe it wasn't a hallucination; that he was actually there, shifting two large heavy suitcases from the doorstep to inside the hall.

He paused only to strip off his wet mac, then came up the stairs two at a time, his grey eyes blazing so fiercely she thought he was going to shake her, shout at her.

But then she was in his arms and he was hugging her so tightly she expected to hear her ribs crack.

'I ought to strangle you,' he said roughly. 'Don't ever do

that to me again! Any problems we have, we'll work out together. I've already solved this one.'

Then he kissed her.

It wasn't until much later, by which time Laurian felt as if she had been through the emotional equivalent of a car-wash, going in downcast and depressed and emerging, breathless and somewhat dishevelled, but glowing with high spirits and happiness, that Oliver explained his solution.

'You remember I told you that from London I went to Spain?'

They were on her big comfortable curly-armed sofa, with Laurian leaning back against a heap of cushions at one end and Oliver looming over her, his black hair ruffled, his shirt collar open.

When she nodded, he went on, 'All over Spain there are hundreds of "ghost" villages . . . places which, for various reasons, have been deserted. Last year I discovered one in the province of Tarragona which I thought had immense possibilities as a new kind of resort. I've been negotiating with one of the Spanish ministries and with various landowners to take possession of the village. If all goes well—and it looks as if it's going to—it will be a project to occupy me for several years.'

'You mean you would move to Europe?'

He nodded. 'From Barcelona to London by air is only a short hop. If we couldn't be together all the time, we should never be apart for long. There's also an airport at Reus, near the city of Tarragona, which is even nearer to the village.'

'Why didn't you mention this before?' asked Laurian.

'There was one possible snag on which the whole plan

hinged. I didn't want to raise your hopes only to dash them. It never occurred to me you wouldn't be there when I got back from Barbados, impetuous girl.'

'And is the snag safely ironed out now?'

'Yes, there was a telex from Spain waiting for me at the Club. All's well. There'll be a thousand and one minor snags to grapple with, but the project is safely off the ground. I was going to go chasing up to Yorkshire after I landed this morning, but I took the precaution of ringing the Lingfields first and Mrs Lingfield told me you'd just left for London. Later I tried your number here several times, but——'

'I've had my answering machine on all day. I didn't feel like talking to anyone,' she told him. There's probably a message from Ma to tell me you rang up.'

'Probably. Anyway, as Robert had given me his key and I had several things to do . . . which reminds me'—Oliver rose from the sofa and crossed the room to where he had slung his tweed jacket—'I decided to attend to them first and then get a taxi here.'

His mention of the Lingfields reminded her of the doctor's warning last night. But she hadn't believed it then and she still didn't.

Oliver came back to the sofa with a small leather box in his hand. Resuming his place close beside her, he opened it.

'If you'd rather design an engagement ring, wear this for the time being and later it will do as a dress ring.'

Without reading the name stamped on the silk lining of the box, Laurian knew the ring he had chosen was by Ilias Lalaounis, the brilliant Greek jewellery designer whose work she had admired in New York and who now had a shop in Bond Street. The ring was from his hand-hammered Seashell Collection which she had already seen and coveted, but had felted was an unreasonable extravagance for her to buy for herself.

Oliver slipped the ring on her finger. 'It's supposed to have been inspired by the inside of a shell, which seemed an appropriate motif for Neptune's daughter,' he said. 'There's a necklace and ear-rings to match, but those I shall give you on our wedding day, which I hope will be as soon as possible.'

'As soon as you like. This is perfect. I adore it. Thank you.' She flung her arms round his neck and scattered half a dozen kisses over his lean brown cheeks and formidable chin.

Later, when it had time to chill, they shared a bottle of champagne which Oliver had had the forethought to buy from a wine merchant on his way through the City.

First they toasted themselves and their future together, and then they drank to the success of the new project in Spain.

'It was time I got something else launched. For a year or two now I've been expecting Archie's successor to appear on the scene,' he said. 'I've been, in effect, a caretaker—although I've done very well out of it. Very well indeed.'

'Archie's successor?' Laurian repeated questioningly.

'Your father devised a rather complicated trust which left the house and the island to his eldest grandson. I was allowed to do what I could with the place and pocket the profits in the interim. If there were any profits, which there might not have been.'

Oliver paused to replenish their glasses. 'You were not to be told officially until your son and his heir was in existence. He had confidence I would make a success of the hotel scheme, which I'd discussed with him, and he didn't want your future husband to be aware, in advance, that he would be getting his hands on a valuable property. However, I always felt Archie was being over-cautious on that point. I felt you'd be happier knowing you still had a stake in the island where you were born. So, that time I saw the Lingfields, I told them about it. As you've never mentioned it, I conclude they shared Archie's view?'

'They told me last night . . . when I told them I was in love with you.'

Laurian thought she would keep to herself their reason for telling her. Soon she and Oliver would be married. Her foster-parents would be the nearest he would come to having in-laws. She hoped it wouldn't be long before they forgot they had ever had reservations about him. Therefore, although she hoped to have few if any secrets from him in the years to come, their suspicions about him she would keep secret.

'I'm a bit surprised Robert lent you his key,' she said. 'How was he when you last saw him?'

'Taking his disappointment on the chin. I introduced him to Mary and she said she'd keep an eye on him. I don't think they have much in common, but you never know.'

'No . . . you never know,' she agreed, watching the bubbles rise in the pale golden wine. 'Who, seeing me stalk out of Fortnum's that afternoon, would dream that a short time later I'd be wearing your ring?'

Oliver came close and stroked her cheek with the back of his knuckles. 'Can we really get married quickly? You don't feel you owe it to your career to design a knock-out wedding dress and have a big public affair?'

'Positively not!' she assured him. 'Let's have a quick, quiet wedding and then disappear to Spain. I can't wait to see this deserted village of yours.'

'What about tonight? May I stay here?'

She pretended to look uncertain. Then she laughed. 'Try and get away!'

They were standing beside a low table. They both leaned to one side to put down their unfinished glasses of champagne. Oliver's arms closed round her waist. Her arms encircled his neck. Locked together, they looked long and lovingly into each other's eyes.

'Do you think perhaps Archie hoped this might happen one day?' she murmured.

'He did once tell me he thought you'd grow up a lovely woman. I wish now I'd checked that out a long time ago.'

As he bent his tall head to hers, Laurian closed her eyes and parted her lips for his kiss.

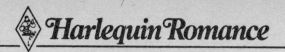
Harlequin Romance

Coming Next Month

2941 WHIRLPOOL OF PASSION Emma Darcy
Ashley finds Cairo fascinating, and even more so the mysterious sheikh she encounters in the casino. She's aware their attraction is mutual, but doesn't take it seriously until he kidnaps her....

2942 THIS TIME ROUND Catherine George
It's all very well for Leo Seymour to want to share her life, Davina thinks, but she can't forget that his first love married her brother years ago. Would Davina's secret love for him be enough to sustain their relationship?

2943 TO TAME A TYCOON Emma Goldrick
It isn't that Laura absolutely doesn't trust tycoon Robert Carlton; she only wants to protect her young daughter from him. And Robert has all his facts wrong about Laura. If there was only some way to change their minds about each other.

2944 AT FIRST SIGHT Eva Rutland
From the time designer Cicely Roberts accidentally meets psychiatrist-author Mark Dolan, her life is turned upside down. Even problems she didn't know she had get straightened out—and love comes to Cicely at last!

2945 CATCH A DREAM Celia Scott
Jess is used to rescuing her hapless cousin Kitty from trouble, but confronting Andros Kalimantis in his lonely tower in Greece is the toughest thing she's ever done. And Kitty hadn't warned her that Andros is a millionaire....

2946 A NOT-SO-PERFECT MARRIAGE Edwina Shore
James's suspected unfaithfulness was the last straw. So Roz turned to photography, left James to his business and made a successful career on her own. So why should she even consider letting him back into her life now?

Available in November wherever paperback books are sold, or through Harlequin Reader Service:

In the U.S.
901 Fuhrmann Blvd.
P.O. Box 1397
Buffalo, N.Y. 14240-1397

In Canada
P.O. Box 603
Fort Erie, Ontario
L2A 5X3

Taylor House

by Leigh Anne Williams

Enter the lives of the Taylor women of Greensdale, Massachusetts, a town where tradition and family mean so much. A story of family, home and love in a New England village.

Don't miss the Taylor House trilogy, starting next month in Harlequin American Romance with #265 *Katherine's Dream*, in October 1988, and followed by #269 *Lydia's Hope* and #273 *Clarissa's Wish* in November and December of 1988.

One house . . . two sisters . . . three generations

Take 4 best-selling love stories FREE
Plus get a FREE surprise gift!

If **YOU** enjoyed this book,
your daughter may enjoy

Romances from

CROSSWINDS

Keepsake is a series of tender, funny, down-to-earth romances for younger teens.

The simple boy-meets-girl romances have lively and believable characters, lots of action and romantic situations with which teens can identify.

Available now wherever books are sold.

ADULT-1